Thomas Morell

Notes and Annotations on Locke on the Human Understanding

Thomas Morell

Notes and Annotations on Locke on the Human Understanding

ISBN/EAN: 9783741186592

Manufactured in Europe, USA, Canada, Australia, Japa

Cover: Foto ©Andreas Hilbeck / pixelio.de

Manufactured and distributed by brebook publishing software
(www.brebook.com)

Thomas Morell

Notes and Annotations on Locke on the Human Understanding

NOTES

AND

ANNOTATIONS

ON

LOCKE

ON

THE HUMAN UNDERSTANDING,

WRITTEN

By ORDER of the QUEEN;

CORRESPONDING IN SECTION AND PAGE WITH THE

EDITION OF 1793.

By THOMAS MORELL, D. D.

RECTOR OF BUCKLAND, & F. S S. R. & A.

LONDON:

Printed for G. SAEL, Newcastle Street, Strand..

1794.

PREFACE,

THE reputation of Mr. Locke is too well known to ftand in need of any eulogium, and every publication tending to elucidate fo valuable a production as his ESSAY on HUMAN UNDERSTANDING, cannot but excite the attention and be worthy the patronage of the *Literati*; more efpecially fo when iffuing from the pen of Dr. Morell, of whom the late Lord Lyttelton has given the following pleafing character:

"He certainly deferves well of, and is "efteemed by, the learned world; but the acute "critic and profound grammarian feems to be "impelled rather by the love of fcience, than "the defire of gain,—is generally in the habit "of frugal contentment, and hides himfelf in "that fhade of retirement, where the learned "few alone can find him. I am, however,

2   "entirely

" entirely of opinion, that he merits a lefs re-
" ftrained fituation than he poffeffes; and I
" cannot forgive Dr. B—— for a breach of
" juftice in oppofing his election to a fellow-
" fhip at Eton. Such a promotion would have
" been a fuitable reward for his labours, and
" have afforded him that ample independence,
" and learned retreat, which would have left
" his clofing life without a wifh."*

The Doctor finifhed his long, well-fpent life
with every tribute due to his memory, when,
amongft other manufcripts in his own hand-
writing, the following *ingenious production* was
found; which, with a part of his valuable li-
brary, came into the poffeffion of the prefent Pub-
lifher, where the *original* may be *feen*; and, with
great propriety, may claim a place as an appen-
dage to the works of Locke lately reprinted.

* See Lord Lyttelton's Letters.

NOTES AND ANNOTATIONS

ON

L O C K E

ON

THE HUMAN UNDERSTANDING,

CORRESPONDING WITH

THE EDITION OF 1793,

BOOK I,

C H A P.   I.

Introduction.

§ 8, *page* 6. IT is the *thing as it exifts in the mind by way of conception or reprefentation,* that is properly called the *Idea,* whether the object be abfent or prefent.*

And accordingly he ufes it fometimes for the thoughts or conceptions themfelves *in* the mind, and fometimes for the things themfelves *without* the mind, that are the objects of its thoughts; and this often in the fame fentence, and without any diftinction; which creates great difficulty in the underftanding his meaning.†

There is no *idea* in the mind, but when it has fome refemblance, picture, image, or likenefs of that which is without it, and never occurs but in that act of the

---

* Watts Log. p. 9.   † Lee, p. 1.

Vol. I,   B   mind

mind which is commonly called *Imagination*; and therefore whenever it is used in any other sense, it is *metaphorical* and *improper.**

· Page 7. Idea nomine intelligo cujuslibet cogitationis formam illam, per cujus immediatam perceptionem ipsius cogitationis ejusdem conscius sum, Adeo ut nihil possim verbis exprimere intelligendo id quod dico, quin ex hoc ipso certum sit, in me esse ideam ejus quod verbis illis significatur. Atque ita non solas imagines in Phantasia depictas ideas voco: imo ipsas hic nullo modo ideas voco, quatenus sunt in Phantasia corporea hoc est, in parte aliqua cerebri depicta, sed quatenus mentem ipsam in illam cerebri partem conversam informant. This is very express and full, agreeably to Mr. Locke's acceptation of the word idea.†

CHAP. II.

No Innate Principles in the Mind.

§ 1, *page* 13. BY *innate speculative principles* are meant such *general* truths as the mind in *all* its reasonings, arguings, and judgements *always* and *necessarily* supposes true, as it does the truth of its own faculties.‡ They are called *Innate*, because as soon as we perceive or judge at all, we cannot but judge their parts have the relation between them, as is expressed in them : *Speculative*, because they do not immediately influence our external actions : *Principles*, because all other propositions, which are more particular, or whose parts are less *common* names than they are, are and must be resolved into *them*, or *identical* propositions as they are themselves, or *negation* of that *identity*, before we can be certain of their truth,

---

* Lee, p. 1.   † Baxt. N. p. 310.
‡ Watts Log. p. 8. Athen. Or. v. 2, 208. Vide Dialogues concerning Innate Principles, &c. 8vo. 1779. M. Rev. May, 1779;

And

And in this fenfe only, I conceive, any thoughts or perceptions can be faid to be *innate*, viz. becaufe the powers or faculties of the mind to form fuch thoughts or perceptions are derived from the Author of *Nature*, operating upon it by *neceffary* caufes; but the *actual* perceptions or thoughts muft be owned to be *acquired*; becaufe they proceed from caufes *extraneous* to the mind itfelf, and this I take to be all this author means, and therein I believe no one will differ from him. But it is to be obferved on the other fide, that befides the *natural* capacities or powers of perceiving, affirming, doubting, &c. with which every intelligent is born, it is born alfo with a *native* aptnefs, inclination, or propenfity of *forming* fome thoughts rather than others; of judging fome propofitions *true* rather than *falfe*; fome actions *good* rather than *bad*; and this without the help of any *words* or any *teaching*. And fuch thoughts and propofitions we call *innate* or *natural*, though there be no fuch *actual* thoughts or propofitions born with the mind itfelf, or which it brings into the world with it. So *Tully* fpeaking of felf-defence or felf-prefervation in favour of *Milo* fays, *Eft hæc non fcripta, fed nata lex ; quam non didicimus, accepimus, leginus : verum ex naturâ ipfâ arripuimus, haufimus, expreffimus ; ad quam non docti, fed facti ; non inftituti, fed imbuti fumus.**

§. 5, *page* 14. If there is any ftrength in this argument, it is thrown away by the author himfelf : who plainly reckons embryos no other than vegetables, infants no better than brutes, and ideots a fort of animals between men and brutes, and therefore if all, that *do* or *can* make any judgement, do judge thefe propofitions true, then *univerfal* confent is fufficiently fecured.†

* Lee.   † Ibid. p. 7.

Implanted senses, inftincts, appetites, paffions, and affections, are a remnant of the old philofophy, which ufed to call every thing innate that it could not account for; and therefore it is to be wifhed they were in one fenfe all eradicated; which was undoubtedly the aim of this excellent book: but it may be obferved, that every argument built upon thefe fenfes, &c. will be equally conclufive, whether they be implanted or acquired.*

§ 16, *page* 21. The reafon of this is, becaufe he perceives the fubject and predicate of the former propofition to be the *fame*, but not fo in the greater number. For as for *ideas* he has no other of two and three than of nineteen and thirty-eight, i. e. none at all; we have no abftract *idea* of any number whatever, not fo much as of *unity.*†

§ 18, *page* 23. The *power* of perceiving the relation between the parts of all propofitions, of the truth of which any one is certain, is equally *innate*; but when we come to exercife that power, the difference is as plainly difcoverable as between perfons, temper, or frame of mind or body.‡

§ 19, *page* 24. *Such lefs, &c.* This I own to be right in all truths acquired by experience, and wholly by the fenfes, but not in fuch as are acquired by the mind's exercifing of its *innate* power of judging and comparing; which does not wholly depend upon the information we receive by our *fenfes.*§

§ 23, *page* 27. I anfwer, only the difpofition or aptnefs to judge of the truth of thofe propofitions

---

* Law on King. p. 88.   † Lee, p. 9.
‡ Lee, p. 10.   § Ibid. p. 9.

rather

rather than the contrary, or to doubt of them, and that is enough to give the propofitions that title, without actual perception of the *particulars.**

§ 27, *page* 30. Children are not *confcious* of, or do not remember thefe principles, yet all their actions are governed by them, and which argues a fenfe or knowledge of them.†

§ 28, *page* 32. All thefe arguments are fo far from convincing me that there are no truths but what are *acquired*, (for that is the whole drift of this chapter) that as it is in painting, and all forts of manufactures, the nearer they come to the imitation of nature, fo in all *acquired*, the nearer they come to thofe *innate* or *natural* truths, the clearer or more certain perception of *identity*, or its *negation*, is the meafure of *certainty*, not the agreement or difagreement in *ideas.*‡

CHAP. III.

No Innate Practical Principles.

§ 1, *page* 33. BY *innate practical principles* are meant fuch propofitions as contain an *immutable obligation* upon all fingle perfons and focieties to conform their *practices* to the fenfe of them. They are called *practical*, becaufe they influence external actions; *propofitions*, becaufe they have all the effential parts of a propofition, viz. fubject, predicate, and copula. They are likewife called *laws*, becaufe they have all the effential parts of a *law*, authority, promulgation, fanction. *Promulgation*, becaufe every one that can judge at all, or can do good or harm, judges them true: *Authority*, becaufe impreffed on our minds by the Author of Nature : *Sanction*, becaufe rewards or punifh-

---

* Lee, p. 8.   † Ibid. p. 10.   ‡ Ibid. p. 11.

ments

ments are *naturally* entailed upon the obfervance or non-obfervance of them.*

§ 1, *page* 33. All *moral* rules are as generally and readily affented to as any *felf-evident fpeculative* principles; and the reafon they have not a conftant effect is, becaufe fome paffions or other overpower thofe *natural* inclinations, but do not deftroy them, no more than other bodies deftroy the natural *conatus* of heavy bodies to defcend, though they hinder the effect at prefent.†

§ 2, *page* 34. If *convenience* be fuch an infeparable and remarkable confequence of the obfervance of that rule, that the worlt of men fee it is their intereft to obferve it; this, one would think, was a good argument, that the connexion between the obfervance of that rule, and that effect of it, was *natural,* and therefore defervedly reckoned a *law of nature.*‡

§ 3, *page* 34. This objection would be of great weight, if men were *pure fpirits,* or only the mafter-piece of *mechanifm;* but as they are *free* agents, and have a fenfe of their own, of moving their own and other bodies within certain limits, &c. I cannot fee any neceffity that their *actions* fhould be the conftant interpreters of their *thoughts,* or why they may not act contrary to thofe *innate* principles of knowledge which they have, or by the violence of paffion be hindered from attending to thofe rules of action which they judge beft. Neither is there any reafon why the law of nature fhould *neceffarily* operate upon minds of men more than human laws, or why their not operating upon all perfons calts a greater blemifh on the Author of

---

* Ibid. p. 11. King de Orig. Mali. Sherlock on a Fut. St. p. 124. Pearfon on the Creed, p. 20. Puffend. Law of Nat. l. 2, c. 3. § 13. Sharrock de fin. p. 168. Cumb. de Leg. Nat.
† Lee, p. 13. ‡ Ibid. p. 15.

Nature, as if he formed them to no purpose, than the non-observance of human laws by any subjects, derogates from the honour of the lawgivers.*

§ 4, *page* 35. There may be occasion indeed to explain the words of a *practical* proposition, (as there may of a *speculative*); but there needs no argument to convince any unprejudiced person of the *fitness* of observing it, after he knows the sense of the words.

This *practical* proposition, *Do as you would be done unto,* carries its own evidence and reasonableness with it: and though it wants *explacation,* yet needs no *proof:* for every one understands, that what is equal in one man's case is equal in another's. †

§ 3, *page* 36. The Christian, Hobbist, and Heathen, may give different reasons, and use *different* expressions to add new force to a law of nature; but needs *none* sufficiently to convince an unprejudiced person of his obligation to observe it, but what the wise Author of Nature has suggested before. And their very agreeing to give *different* reasons shews, that nature *operates equally* in them all, in disposing them to use such enforcements. ‡

§ 6, *page* 36. The *profitableness* of virtue rather proves it is *innate;* for where an effect is *constant,* there the cause is the Author of Nature. We do not pretend that the laws of nature so *irresistibly operate* as to make men wise and honest against their wills, but only *incline* them to be such, for their own interest, security, and happiness. *Hypocrisy* proves that it is most *natural* to be really good. §

§ 7, *page* 37. Men's actions convince us indeed that all men are not so good as to govern themselves

* Lee, p. 16. † Ibid. p. 16. ‡ Ibid. p. 17. § Ibid. p. 18.

by the *natural* sense they have of what is good : but not that those persons do not act contrary to their own consciences, unless we can suppose every man as good as he *knows* himself obliged to be.*

§ 8, *page* 38. Education, custom, company, and human laws, may add *new* force to the laws of nature; but if there be no foundations laid in the constitution of our natures, for the distinction between virtue and vice *antecedent* to them, I doubt they will prove but *weak* and *uncertain*, because they will depend upon contingent causes ; and the consequence of this doctrine will prove very *dangerous* to the foundation of *morality* and *natural religion*. But though false notions in religion may go a great way to corrupt men's manners and tempers, yet we never heard of any that were so far corrupted as to own it lawful to kill an innocent person, or break any law of nature merely out of *conscience*. It is not. *conscience*, (whatever is pretended) but some *irregular passion*, mingled with *religious phrenzy*, that oftentimes proves so venomous and mischievous.†

§ 9, *page* 38. Admitting these practices to be true, yet they do not prove that these people were *wholly ignorant* of the laws of nature, only that they were such monsters of men as not to *regard and attend* to them as they ought ;‡ besides, in all these instances, there is no mention of any laws of the country to oblige the people to these enormities. It is one thing *not to punish* or *allow* another to *command* or *reward*. But suppose they were commanded, yet that would not demonstrate that they *knew no better*. There is a famous instance to the contrary in the *Romans* expedition against *Cyprus*. And therefore to make any of these practices

---

* Lee, p. 18.   † Ibid. p. 19.
‡ See this objection answered in § 11.

a convincing

a convincing argument againſt *innate* principles of morality and religion, there muſt be proof, that the perſons who committed them were under no prejudices,
under the power of no paſſions, fear, or hopes of more
preſent advantages or diſadvantages than what nature
ſuggeſts for the contrary practices.

For the whole ſtate of the queſtion is, not whether
men *can* act contrary to theſe *principles* or not ; for in
that point there is no diſpute : nor whether they be
ſtamped upon the ſouls of all men as ſoon as they are
united to their bodies ; that is an idle thing to talk for
or againſt ; but whether human nature be not ſo con-
ſtituted by the wiſe Author of it, as to be more inclined
to the obſervance of ſome rules of action, for the pro-
moting their own, and the happineſs of mankind,
than the breach of them ; or in other words, whether all
men, or any one man, is *free* from all *ſenſe* of duty, and
indifferent to all ſorts of actions ? And I appeal to the
ſenſe of mankind, whether they do not feel, within
themſelves, an *inclination* to one, and an *abhorrence* to
the other ſort of actions, ſuch as are here mentioned ;
and this *abhorrence* I call natural conſcience, and is a de-
monſtration, that we are all born with an inclination to
the obſervance of thoſe rules we call the laws of nature.*

§ 10, *page* 40. This may be owned true, and
yet be no good proof that thoſe rules of morality
are not founded in nature, unleſs it be proved, that
thoſe people who do or have ſlighted them, have, all
things conſidered, fared the *better* for it.†

§ 13, *page* 43. I allow there is ſuch a thing,
which may be called a *moral ſenſe*, in the mind, which
inclines a man to judge right, and eſpecially in the
more general, plain, and obvious queries about virtue

* Lee, p. 21. † Ibid. p. 23.

and vice: But this moral sense is still the same thing: It is intelligence or reason itself, considered as capable of discerning, discoursing, or judging about moral subjects. And it contains the plain and general principles of morality, not explicitly as propositions, but only as native principles, and cannot but judge virtue to be fit, and vice unfit, for intelligent and social creatures whom God hath made.*

§ 14, *page* 44. As for *practical* propositions there are so many of them as there are *moral* rules for *human* actions; in the observance of which, the natural happiness of mankind in general, and of every individual person, all things considered, is promoted, and which every one does, and must know, that knows any thing. And we call them *the laws of nature*, because, in the common course of the world, there are rewards or punishments annexed to the observance or breach of them, antecedent to human laws, and are therefore derivable from no less or other cause, than the Author of Nature, the cause of all necessary effects. And that there are such *laws of nature*, is manifest from these reasons:

1st, Were there no such *immutable* laws of nature, antecedent to all human institutions, all actions would be in themselves *indifferent*.

2d, From the *consciousness* some emperors and princes have of their *evil* actions, when they knew themselves out of the reach of human penalties.

3d, From nature's powerful efficacy in vicious persons at the approach of death.

4th, Some laws of nature seem to have a deeper root than mere custom, education, or the hopes of human rewards, or fears of human punishments, could plant; because human laws themselves derive their whole or

* Watts Eff. p. 111.

main

main ftrength from thofe very laws of nature, and are more or lefs valid as they are more or lefs agreeable to thofe natural laws, or fooner or later refolved into them.*

CHAP. IV.

Other Confiderations concerning Innate Principles, both Speculative and Practical.

§ 1, *page 55.* THERE is no need of *ideas,* i. e. of an actual knowledge of prefent thoughts of the fubject and predicate in general propofitions, to the forming a certain judgement of their truth, but only a *readinefs* of mind to affent to them as foon as the things fignified by the words are propofed ; and to form them into verbal propofitions, as foon as the words are underftood. And becaufe that *power* in the mind of comparing its own thoughts is *natural* to all intelligent beings, and that there is no need of the information of any of our fenfes concerning all the particulars implied in thofe *general* words, therefore fuch propofitions may be called *innate.*†

§ 2, page 55. As for children's not having *ideas,* or notions which *anfwer the terms which make up thofe general propofitions,* it is nothing to the purpofe, for grown men cannot have any fuch ideas. No man can have *ideas* of all the wholes in the world, and of all the parts of thofe wholes ; yet a child that knows, or can judge of any thing, can certainly know and judge, that all wholes are bigger than any one of its parts ; and fo of all other *innate* truths.‡

§ 8, page 57. By the *idea* of God is meant, the notion we have of a being diftinct from ourfelves, and every other *finite* being ; the infinitely wife, good, and powerful *Author* of *Nature,* or *primary* caufe of all *neceffary* effects in the univerfe. And fuch an *idea,* or notion of God, may be called *innate,* becaufe it is formed in the minds of men, without any *teaching,* or *artificial* arguments, or fo much as the knowledge of words, by the efficacy of natural caufes operating upon us, and the unavoidable obfervation of fuch effects as can proceed from no lefs or other caufe, than fuch as we all mean by the word *God.**

The ancients recorded for Atheifts, are *Protagoras, Diagoras, Melius, Theodorus Cyrenaicus,* &c.   But *Tully,* in the very period in which he gives us their names, makes the *belief* of a God *natural* to all men, *quo omnes duce natura vehimur ;* and *Seneca* fays, mentiuntur qui dicunt fe non fentire Deum effe; nam etfi tibi affirment interdiu, noctu tamen, et fibi dubitant.   And Epicurus, that took fo much pains to free himfelf and others of their *natural* fears of God, is reprefented by his cotemporaries, to have been one of the moft *fearful* men in the world, of death, and the gods.

It is fcarce poffible to know the fenfe of whole nations in their difowning the exiftence of God, or to know they had no name for the *natural* notion of God, unlefs we were to fpeak with every fingle perfon, or underftood every fingle word of their language, which is impracticable.   Their having mean and unworthy thoughts of God, is no proof they had no thoughts of God any more than it does that our common people have none of the fun, becaufe they judge it not much bigger than the crown of their hats.†

Deos effe inter alia fic colligimus, quod omnibus de diis opinio infita eft; nec ulla gens ufquam eft adeo extra leges morefque projecta, ut non aliquos deos credat.‡

---

* Lee, p. 29. § 8, Baxt. 241.   † Lee, p. 34. . ‡ Ep. 117.

§ 9, *page* 57. If every man did neceſſarily feel light and heat, as he is conſcious of his own exiſt-ence, then he would as naturally infer that there were ſome ſuch things as we call the ſun and fire, as he that is conſcious of his own exiſtence infers from thence the exiſtence of ſomething diſtinct from, and ſuperior to himſelf; and extending his thoughts to other effects of the viſible world, he enlarges his thoughts concern-ing the nature and perfections of God by ſuch *natural* and *unavoidable* impreſſions from external objects, with-out the help of teaching or words, as he may do of the fire or the ſun, by ſuch *natural* effects which come from ſuch cauſes.*

§ 14, *page* 98. However the Heathen world dif-fered from each other in the nature and number of their inferior deities, and in their cuſtoms, languages, and modes of worſhip, yet they all agreed in this that there was *one God*, the cauſe or ſupreme Author of Nature, and of all happineſs and calamities, which is the moſt obvious and natural notion of God.†

§ 19, *page* 69. The ſimple ideas of light, colours, ſounds, &c. even all *ſenſible* qualities (or *ſecondary* qua-lities of bodies) though they are not immediately, ac-tually and implicitly impreſſed at once upon the mind, at its firſt union to the body, yet they may in ſome ſenſe be called *innate :* for they ſeem given to the mind by a divine energy, or law of union between ſoul and body, appointed in the firſt creation of man. And this law operates, or begins its efficacy in all particular inſtances, as ſoon as thoſe ſenſible objects occur, which give occaſion to theſe ſenſible qualities and ideas to be firſt perceived by the mind.

So ſome principles of knowledge (though not ex-plicit propoſitions) may be in a ſenſe *innate* alſo,—

* Lee, p. 34.   † Ibid. p. 35.

though

though they are not actually inscribed on the mind of man in its first formation, yet the very nature, make and frame of a rational mind is such, that it cannot but judge according to such axioms, as *whatsoever* acteth hath a being, &c. They are, (as Mr. Glanvil calls them) the very essentials of rationality : and if any one ask how the soul came by them, I answer, as *quantity* did by length, breadth, and depth.*

Therefore I take the mind or soul of men not to be so perfectly indifferent to receive all impressions, as a rasa tabula, or white paper, &c.†

§ 20, *page* 69. It is full as easy to conceive how the Author of our Natures in the frame of our souls and bodies, may make it easy and natural to judge a proposition true, as soon as the words of it are understood, though we had not before any *actual* knowledge of the subject and predicate, as it is to make us reperceive or remember any thing, which we have not in our thoughts at that instant.‡

BOOK II.   CHAP. I.

Of Ideas, *in General, and their Original.*

§ 2, *page* 77. IT is commonly thought, that the minds of men come by all their knowledge either by the immediate exercise of their own *natural powers,* in their several manners of operation about their several objects : or 2, by testimony *human* or *divine.*

The 1st *natural* power is sensation, i. e. the perception of those impressions which are made by *external* objects upon the several organs of the body framed for that purpose.

* Vide the Vanity of Dogmatizing, p. 8:.
† Watts Eff. p. 106.   ‡ Lee, p. 36.

The

The 2d is *imagination*, or the power of exciting in our minds the idea of any sort of object, which we have either seen ourselves before, or has been reprefented by others as vifible or fenfible.

The 3d is *underftanding*, which is only the power of exciting in our minds, thoughts of things by articulate founds, words written, or other fenfible marks, and by the diligent exercife of this we acquire *wifdom.**

The 4th is the *natural* power of judging, i. e. the comparing of thofe objects we have perceived or imagined, and by obferving their agreement or difagreement with one another, we form propofitions either negative or affirmative, modal or general.

The 5th is that of *reafoning*, which is the inferring the truth of *one* propofition from *another*, by obferving the relation in which either of the terms of one propofition ftands to another.

The 6th is *memory*, or the facility of thinking of a thing which we thought on before,† and the confciouf-nefs of what is thus perceived, imagined, underftood, compared, inferred, or remembered, is what moft men call *knowing*, or in the general fenfe of the *underftanding*.‡

§ 3, 4, vide note on § 24, *p.* 91, concerning fenfation and reflection, *page* 78. Though the firft original of ideas may be entirely owing to thefe two principles, fenfation and reflection; yet the recollection and frefh ex-citation of them may be owing to a thoufand other oc-cafions and occurrences in life.§

We obtain the knowledge of a multitude of propo-fitions as well as of fingle ideas by thofe two principles which Mr. Locke calls fenfe and reflection.‖ One of them is a fort of confcioufnefs of what affects the body, and the other of what affects the mind. Propofitions

---

* Proceed. of the Underft. b. 3, c. 4. Jac. *Ode* Theol. Nat. p. 39. Watts Eff. p. 115.
† Vide Watts Eff. p. 75. ‡ Lee, p. 40.
§ Watts Log. p. 30. ‖ Watts Eff. p. 75.

which

which are built on this internal confcioufnefs, have yet
no particular or diftinguifhing name affigned to them.*

§ 5, *page* 79. The firft of thefe propofitions is clear
enough : the fecond is not fo. By the *mind*, he muft mean
the *thinking fubftance* ; by the *underftanding*, the *perceptive faculty* ; by *ideas, perceptions* ; by *operations*, the *actions* and *paffions* of the mind. So that in the other
propofition runs thus, the *thinking fubftance* furnifhes
the *thinking faculty* with the thoughts of its own
thoughts : by all which he intends no more than this,
that the mind is confcious of its own actions and
paffions.†

§ 6, *page* 79. But it is as obfervable, that as the
objects increafe upon them in variety, fo the power of
perceiving them does, and that power has another
fource befides the *objects* themfelves : unlefs what we
call *perception,* as in the mind, be nothing but what we
call *motion* in the object.‡

§ 7, *page* 80. No one doubts this; but the queftion
is, whether the *perceptive faculties* grow or be mul-
tiplied *purely* by the efficacy of the objects themfelves,
or acquired only from that caufe, or a fuperior?
Though the brain be the organ of the memory, yet it
does not itfelf any more remember than the eye fees :
and whatever motions may precede, accompany or
follow imagination and reafoning; yet if there be not
fome one certain fubftance, call it the foul or what you
pleafe, that perceives all thefe various motions, that
unites thofe various perceptions, that compares them
upon occafion, that is confcious of all thefe tranfactions,
they would perifh the next moment, and the mind itfelf would be no more capable of *variety* in knowledge,

* Watts Log. p. 179.   † Lee, p. 44.   ‡ Ibid.

than

than a piece of foft wax is of *different* impreffions at the *fame* inftant.*

§ 10, *page* 81. *That actual thinking, &c.* The ftrength of all the *Cartefian* arguments to prove that *thinking* includes the *effential* or *diftinguifhing* property of a fpirit, may be reduced to this one fyllogifm, and will be very difficult to find a reafon to deny either of the propofitions.†

That *with* which we may have a *clear* and *diftinct* notion of a fpirit, and *without* which we can have *no* notion of it at all, is the *effential* property of a fpirit.

But *thinking* is that *with* which, &c.—*Ergo,*

§ 10, *page* 81. It is very improper to refer to *experience* in this cafe,‡ viz. for the reality of a ftate, which by fuppofition is an utter negation of all experience.

§ 10, *page* 81, *line* 11. But with fubmiffion, there is this material difference, motion is no more the action of matter than reft is, it is equally inactive in both. Matter ftands in need of an external caufe to put it in motion or bring it to reft again, but the foul does not want an external mover to fet it a thinking. And therefore there is no room to run a comparifon between the action of the foul, which neceffarily fprings out of its own nature, and the motion of matter, which muft be excited in it by fome being not material. This looks as if action was really extrinfic to them both; or as if it were as natural for the foul to be without action, as for matter to be without motion, which is to pervert our jufteft conceptions of fpiritual fubftance.§

If we *take away from our idea,* or deny activity and perceptivity concerning fpiritual fubftance, by which we can only collect it to be a fubftance, we deny every

---

* Lee, p. 44.   † Vide Baxt. p. 144, 152.   Vide Inf. 154.
‡ Vide Infr. p. 184.   Baxt. p. 145.   § Ibid. p. 146.

thing we know concerning it, or we deny ourselves to have any idea of it; and reasoning about it as without those powers, we reason precisely about nothing, of which we have any particular idea.   To say it may still be a substance without these powers, is to suppose it *dead substance*, which could never come to the exercise of these powers again, if it had once lost them, as we see it doth.   And therefore it can never be without them. *

Besides allowing Mr. Locke's acceptation of the word essence (3, 3, 15) it will not follow that every thing is separable from substances, which is not this real internal constitution as he seems to take for granted. The properties that immediately flow from the internal constitution of things are as inseparable from them as that constitution itself, and we can as little conceive the thing without these properties, as without that constitution. †

§ 10, *page* 81. *I confess myself, &c.* This *modesty*, which is designed for an argument, is somewhat inaccurate, for he confesses a thing for certain which he can never be certain of.   It is not in the power of the soul to become impercipient of ideas at pleasure; and were the thing effected, it would be the sign of an ill-disposed body, and not of the dullness of the soul.

It is true the argument is good, that a man cannot think at any time, waking or sleeping, without being sensible of it, but this respects the present time, and is far from concluding that a man cannot think sleeping or waking without retaining the memory of such thoughts, which yet is the thing designed to be concluded by it.   Why else should experience be alledged, which is the memory of things past? ‡

§ 10, *page* 81. *But I do say, &c.* This seems to be granting the inference he so much dreads; for if the

---

* Baxt. p. 145.   † Ibid. p. 146.   ‡ Ibid. p. 148.

soul

soul does not *think* when the man is afleep, we can have no reafon to fay that it *exifts*; becaufe we fay that of a thing of which we have *no notion* at all, we fay fomething of that of which, fo far as we know, is *nothing*; and *nihili nullæ funt affectiones.**

§ 10, *page* 81. The queftion here is rather about a matter of *not fact*, about a negation of all fact. Every body- allows we are generally confcious. It is abfurd to fay, we forget our unconfcioufnefs, or we remember our unconfcioufnefs. Where is the matter of fact to be teftified to them; or how is experience applicable? Let a definition of experience be given.†

§ 10, *page* 81. *It is hardly to be conceived that, &c.* If this argument proved any thing, it would prove too much; for it would prove, *we never dream.* For, I prefume, all men's dreams are alike incoherent and *ufelefs*; but fuch as they are, they are of ufe to prove, we may have *ufelefs* thoughts, without any affront to the Majefty of our Creator.‡

§ 11, *page* 83. Sleep not an affection of the whole man.§
The foul acts not by itfelf fo as to be a different perfon.‖

§ 11, *page* 83. As to *confcioufnefs*, it is impoffible to prove or difprove it directly. It is probable that the mind,. though there be a ceffation of the *external* organs of *fenfe*, may perceive a conftant *pleafure* in found fleep, from the perpetual *fteam of fpirits* that are rifing from the circulation of the blood, efpecially fince that motion muft needs be even and regular in found fleep, or from other caufes: and people fuddenly

---

* Lee, p. 45.   † Baxt. p. 148. Vide p. 184.   ‡ Lee, p. 47.
§ Baxt. p. 199,   ‖ Ibid. p. 291.

awakened find a kind of *reluctancy*, at that inftant, to be deprived of that *pleasure.* This I confefs cannot be demonftrated, but much lefs the contrary ; and there is this to be added to the probability of it, that our very dreams which we do remember, and the imagination we often have in them of *vifible* objects, much *clearer* than awake, do manifeftly evince that the perceptive princi-ple in us does not wholly depend upon the external fenfes, for the exercife of all its natural powers ; but can per-form fome of them without fuch a monitor, efpecially without being rid by the violence of *external* objects.*

§ 11, *page* 83. Who can fay that he ever found himfelf in a ftate of unconfcioufnefs ? It is contradic-tory that any man fhould fo furprize himfelf with refpect to the time prefent ; and as to the paft time, he cannot have any memory of fuch a ftate ; for whether ever fuch a ftate was or was not, it is either way a con-tradiction that he fhould remember it, and he cannot bring an argument for it from his not remembering of it.   He did not perceive an abfence of confcioufnefs then ; nor can he now: fince he could only do it by remembrance.   He hath not two diftinct confciouf-nefles, one to be extinguifhed, and another remaining to perceive the abfence of the firft.†

It is ftrange if any man put him to the trouble of confuting this contradiction, with the fuppofition of Caftor and Pollux, Socrates and Plato.   The pofition his adverfaries maintain, infers no fuch contradiction, nor juftifies another to infer it for them.   There is cer-tainly a great deal of our paft confcioufnefs, which we retain no memory of afterward.   It is a particular mark of our finite and imperfect natures, that we can-not become confcious of all our paft confcioufnefs at pleafure.   But no man at night would infer, that he was not in a ftate of confcioufnefs and thinking at fuch

* Lee, p. 46.   † Vide Baxt. p. 147.

a certain time of day, becaufe now, perhaps, he hath no memory what particular thought he had at that minute. And it is no better argument confidered in itfelf, that a man was not confcious at fuch a minute in his fleep, becaufe next morning he hath no memory of what ideas were in his mind then.*

§ 11, *page* 83. It is here granted, that while we are awake, we are under the neceffity of thinking; how comes it then we are not always awake? Is it the defect of the foul? This was the chief point to be confidered. But fpirit hath no parts, and therefore ftands in no need of reparation or re-difpofing its parts aright, as the body doth, which confifts of parts which are conftantly changing, and liable to be difordered; this fhews on which fide the indifpofition lies.†

§ 12, *page* 84. A man afleep may perceive, or think, and be confcious of it at that inftant, and yet not retain the thoughts of it when awake; and that too without being, to all effects and purpofes, two different perfons for want of that memory. For if the want of memory was a fufficient reafon to make different perfons, then the fame man might be an hundred men in the fame day, by forgetting his feveral fucceeding thoughts within that time. The fuppofition therefore of Caftor's foul in Pollux's body while afleep, is a little too romantic; but it is levelled againft the belief of fome that the foul is a diftinct fubftance from the body, and therefore, as he infers, may act apart; but as diftinct fubftances as they are, yet there is a mutual communication between the *thoughts* of the foul and the *motions* of the body;‡ but the foul of one man can no more be in another man's body than one man can be confcious of another's thoughts, or feel his pain with the gout.§

* Vide Baxt. p. 149.　† Ibid. p. 75.
‡ Baxt. p. 115.　§ Lee, p. 47.

§ 12, *page* 84. When we fall heavy with sleep, or sink from waking to a sleeping state, we lose gradually the perception of external objects or whatever we were thinking of, as the mind ceases to be active in applying the attention to them, till all degenerates into an internal scene of thinking, where the mind is still active, and perceptive of and about other objects.*

I cannot help being concerned to find some great and learned men taking the wrong side of ambiguous appearances, and falling in with the sceptical notions of the world, by insinuating, that the soul owes the perfection of rational thinking to the body ; and this in order to maintain another hypothesis of no very great consequence in itself though it were true in this state of union, viz. that the soul thinks not always, which yet is not easily to be proved, even though the activity of spirit be clogged with dead matter, and is certainly false in a state of separation.†

§ 14, *page* 85. If we consider the temper of the brain, while we are fast asleep, partly by the plentiful resort of the animal spirits which used to be otherwise employed, partly by the continual recruit which sleep was designed to make ; it cannot be conceived otherwise, but there must be a very quick succession of thought, and continual interfering and crossing of those spirits in their motions, and thereby hindering one another from making any distinct impressions in the brain, which is doubtless the chief organ of memory. And what the variety of succeeding objects may do whilst awake, that much more the various and multiform motion of the animal spirits may do whilst asleep. And let a man be never so suddenly awaked, the very concussion of the nerves (if by external violence) communicated to the brain may shatter, and confound and blot out, in that moment, all the impressions which the

* Bax', p. 198.   † Ibid. p. 142.

thoughts

thoughts had made before, and if awaked without any such foreign force, the sudden and hasty motion of the spirits to the external parts may work the like effect.*

§ 14, *page* 85. This objection is not rightly stated. It is not only possible, but easy to forget on being awakened, what we were dreaming the minute before. And due care being taken, it is certainly also not impossible to observe it in many cases. A very remarkable author writing on this subject, saith, " I suppose the soul is never totally inactive. I never awaked since I had the use of my memory, but I found myself coming out of a dream. And I suppose they that think they dream not, think so because they forget their dreams."†

§ 16, *page* 87. If the soul were indebted to matter for the perfection of rational thinking, matter would be the more perfect being of the two. And if thinking, or activity does not belong to the nature of immaterial substance; it must be merely accidental to all substance, which is no less absurd.‡

Again, we have undoubted experience that the soul thinks and lives, while the senses are shut up and can minister nothing; and lastly, allowing all that is alledged, viz. that sometimes we sleep without dreaming, is it therefore to be inferred that sleep is an affection of the soul? Is it not conceivable to any man of common sense, that its activity may be quite hindered from being exerted, and its perceptivity entirely impeded, without supposing it to be laid up to be refitted, in sleep, as the body is, or making sleep an affection of a material being.§

In a dream, when it is certain that the soul is percipient and awake, it is yet not percipient of any external

---

* Baxt. p. 47.   † Mr. R. B. on the Soul's Immortality.
‡ Baxt. p. 143.   § Ibid. p. 153.

touch upon the body: Why? Becaufe the action is really not communicated to it. Hence is manifeft on which fide the indifpofition lies, and that fleep is not an affection of the whole man, foul as well as body, as Mr. Locke infinuates.*

§ 16, *page* 87. Here is a broad hint for material fouls.—What is *for the moft part only*, is not always ; that fide ought alfo to have been confidered.† But the moft incoherent of our dreams is an appearance far above matter, or any power matter can be endued with: and upon a narrow examination the actions properly of the foul in dreaming will not be found fo irrational as is here prefumed, and generally conceived.‡

This abfurdity, (that the foul, &c.) is firft made a confequence of what thefe men fay, and immediately it is furmifed that the quality of our dreams fhews this abfurdity to be fact.§ This is really a ftrange way of proceeding, to fhuffle over the odioufnefs of an infinuation upon, and in cafe they fhould difown it, and that circumftance from which he would infer it (viz. that the foul thinks without being confcious of it) to endeavour to prove it, by an appearance, which is ready at hand. Thefe men deny that the foul thinks lefs or more rationally, without being confcious of it, and therefore any confequence of fuch a pofition ; but who is it here that appeals to the frivoloufnefs and irrationality of dreams to fhew that the foul owes the perfection of rational thinking to the body. Mr. Locke fhould have told us what were his own fentiments of this affair ; and if it were an abfurdity, fhewn us how it was to be avoided ; but firft to endeavour to turn it over to his as fomething very unjuftifiable, which therefore fhewed the abfurdity of their opinion, and then to endeavour to prove it, was altogether fingular. Here he fuppofes

* Baxt. p. 155.   † Ibid. p. 174, 181.
‡ Ibid. p. 143.   § Ibid. 270, 274.

that

that the foul itfelf produces all it hears and fees in fleep, that it thinks apart and feparately at that time, and exerts the utmoft perfection it is capable of, when deftitute of the help of the body. How unjuft and inaccurate a reprefentation of this appearance is this.*

This obfervation of Mr. Locke is fo far from being exact, that if he had made juft the contrary obfervation, it would have been equally true, which is remarkable enough in a man of his accuracy and judgement. Befides, how could the foul upon Mr. Locke's own principles form to itfelf in fleep a fcene of our waking actions and thoughts, and the man be ftill ignorant of it, without being two diftinct perfons ?† If a lawyer anfwers the objections of the oppofite party in his fleep, and if he made thefe objections againft himfelf, fhould he not be as confcious that he made them, as that he made the anfwers to them ? If objections are made, the efficiency of a rational intelligent caufe is interefted, from the nature of the inftance : and if the perfon himfelf anfwers the objections, the foul reafons fometimes in fleep, or *hath ideas under the conduct of the underftanding.*‡

From our intimacy and acquaintance with this, vifion, however new and ftrange to us, it is plain that the foul is capable of a more perfect and ready knowledge of things than that which it attains to now by the methods of fenfe and reflection.§

§ 24, *page* 91. The reflecting of the mind upon its own operations can fignify nothing to the increafe of knowledge, unlefs we be improved in our knowledge of thofe things on which we have thought. If the mind has not *innate* powers of carrying its thoughts further than the fenfes, it will be never the better furnifhed by reflecting or viewing what it has gained thereby : the

* Baxt. p. 270. † Vide Lucret. 4, p. 960.
‡ Baxt. p. 276. § Ibid. p. 292.

operations themselves will not afford a new set of *ideas*, for they are only the *modes of thinking* so named; of which we have no ideas at all, when abstracted from the objects about which they are employed. And if this author means any thing more by *reflexion*, then it is the same which every body means by *knowing*, and it is very improper to reck'on that to be a source of *knowledge*, which is *knowing itself*; and therefore he might as well have said in *Gassendus's* words, *nihil est intellectu, quod non prius fuit in sensu*. And therefore what he is pleased to call *natural* must be *acquired* (if all knowledge be) from our *senses* too. And if that be his meaning I conceive a *sensation*, an inadequate original of all knowledge, imperfect as it is, for these reasons:

1st, Because our external senses do, or can give no true account, or near it, so much as of *corporeal* substances, or of any one of their *modes*.

2dly, Our *senses* must be infinitely defective as to *immaterial* substances; for into them the senses can give us no insight at all.

3dly, There are several general propositions as certainly true, as that our faculties are not deceived, yet we can come at no knowledge of them *merely* by our senses; because they cannot reach to all the particulars included in the subjects of them.

And lastly, There are some propositions as certainly true as that the sun is a luminous body; and yet the terms which constitute them, cannot be understood by the senses; as where the subject is a *negative*, *nihil nullæ sunt affectiones*, or nothing cannot produce an effect. No one will say he has an *idea* of nothing by his *senses*. Whatever *natural powers therefore the mind has, neither they* nor the exercise of them, can be derived from the sensation of external objects; but must come, by insensible ways, from the Author of nature in the constitution of our souls; and it is as rational to believe, that these *natural* powers are gradually imparted

to

to the foul according to its fucceffive capacities to exercife them, as that the foul itfelf was at firft *created* by
the *infinitely-wife* Author.*

CHAP. II.

Of Simple IDEAS.

§ 1, *page* 93. *SOME of them are fimple, &c.* But the
better to underftand this difference,
he fhould have given fome mark or definition of them,
that fo we might diftinguifh them from one another.†
But we muft be content with amplification inftead of
definition, which is a tedious, and I fear we fhall not
find a fafer way to knowledge.‡

Thefe qualities that affect our fenfes, when in the
mind, are mere perceptions, and thofe perceptions have
none of the features of the qualities themfelves, as he
himfelf exprefsly owns, and therefore cannot with any
propriety be called *ideas*, much lefs *fimple ideas*.§

As a man fees at once, &c. I queftion whether the fight can
take in at once colour and motion diftinctly; for though
the fucceffion in the acts of perception are very quick,
yet, I doubt, that if there were not diftinct inftants, the
perceptions of them could never be fo; however this is
certain they can never be perceived diftinctly from that
body in which they are, and fo are *complex perceptions*,
or *ideas*.‖

A fimple idea is one uniform idea, which cannot be
divided or diftinguifhed by the mind of man into two
or more ideas.¶

§ 3, *page* 96. What our author fays is *poffible*, feems
moft *certain*, that *fuperior* intelligent beings have other

* Baxt. p. 43. † Vide Watts Log. p. 33. ‡ Lee, p. 48.
§ Lee, p. 48. ‖ Ibid. p. 49. ¶ Watts Log. p. 33.
VOL. I, E 2 organs

organs for fenfations than we have, and for memory
than a *brain* fuch as we have; otherwife it would be
naturally impoffible, that angels and fouls feparated
from their *prefent* bodies fhould have any memory of
their *paft* actions, or perceptions of *greater* pleafure or
pain than we now have.*

CHAP. IV.
Of Solidity.

§ 1, *page* 99. THE word Solid is generally ufed in
contradiftinction to hollownefs, fig-
nifying confiftency, continuity, or mutual coherence of
parts, and fometimes hardnefs; which is no pofitive but
a relative quality to the conftitution of our bodies, and
therefore not fo fit to be fet up for the effential property of a body as extenfion, which of late has had the
name of it.†

§ 3, *page* 100.   *Space* diftinct from *Body*:‡ for *space*
feems to be the general name of what immediately
affects our fenfes only with extenfion: body, the general
name of what affects our fenfes with either figure, motion, or reft, befides extenfion.§

CHAP. V.
Of Simple IDEAS of divers Senfes.

Page 104. IF there be any fpace beyond the confines
of body, we cannot have fo much as the
conception of it, but only by the exercife of *reafon*, inferring that there may be fuch *fpace*, becaufe we cannot

* Watts Log. p. 49.   † Ibid. p. 50.
‡ Vide c. 13, § 11, p. 152.   § Lee, p. 71.

2   imagine

imagine or invent any *external* cauſe that ſhould hinder the infinite extenſion of the univerſe, but that is not an idea, but a *rational* inference.*

C H A P. VI.

Of Simple IDEAS *of Reflection.*

§ 2, *page* 104. HOW *thinking* comes to be placed to *perception* only needs explication, for when we will love, hate, or deſire, we *think*, as well as when we underſtand, imagine, or judge.†

C H A P. VII.

Of Simple IDEAS *of both Senſation and Reflection.*

§ 1, *page* 105. BUT what notion can a man have of *pleaſure* or *pain* alone, I mean, without conſidering the *cauſes* of them, or *ſubjects* wherein they are? So that *pleaſure* and *pain* ſeem only the names of our perceptions; *power*, *unity*, and *exiſtence* the names only of the acts of the mind itſelf, exerciſed about things operating, exiſting, and being one, and not any abſtract *ideas* or *objects* of the mind.‡

C H A P. VIII.

Some farther Conſiderations concerning our Simple IDEAS.

§ 1, *page* 109. THE cauſe of all perceptions is ſomething *real* or *poſitive*; for in plain Engliſh, a *privative* cauſe, or the *privation* of a cauſe, is *no cauſe* at all.§

---

* Lee, p. 53.   † Ibid.   ‡ Ibid. p. 54.   § Ibid.

§ 7, *page* 111, *line* 6.   That fo *we may not think*.—
That the old philofophers thought fo, appears from
their giving the fame name to the *quality* in the body,
that excites a fenfation in us, and to the fenfation excited as, *Calor in igne, homo Calidus*.

When a thought is raifed in our mind by the action
of fome real thing without us, this *idea* is the effect of
a *pofitive* caufe: but it often happens that a new thought
fhall arife from the want of a real thing, or when it
ceafes to act; here is a *privative* caufe.

§ 8, *page* 111.   Idea, what.—The *form* under which
things appear to the mind or the refult of our conception or apprehenfion, is called an *idea*.*

Which ideas.   This ufe of the word *idea*, viz. for
the quality producing it, will be apt to mifguide any
one that does not remember this admonition.†

Primary qualities are fuch as belong to bodies confidered in themfelves, whether there was any man to
take notice of them or no.‡

§ 11, *page* 113.   In the act of *imagination* indeed,
when the object is not prefent, there is an *idea* of the
vifible object in the mind itfelf: but whether it be fo,
when the object is actually prefent, is not fo evident;
becaufe we cannot eafily diftinguifh between the impreffion which is properly the act of the *object*, and the
perception which is the act of the *mind*.§   But this is
certain, that there is at no time an idea or perception of
any of thofe qualities *without* the fubject in which they
are, and fo there can be no fuch things as *fimple ideas*,
they are all *compounded*.||

Secondary qualities are fuch ideas as we afcribe to
bodies on the account of various impreffions which are
made on the fenfes of men by them.¶

---

* Watts Log. p. 5.   ¶ § 9, Ibid. p. 24.   ‡ Ibid.
‡ Watts Eff. p. 105. || Lee, p. 56.   ¶ Watts Log. p. 24.

§ 15, *page* 114, *line* 5. *But the ideas produced in us by these secondary qualities.* Becaufe when the *ideas of the secondary qualities* are produced, there is nothing more in the bodies, than when the *ideas of the primary qualities* were produced : there is only a determinate fet, or combination of the *primary qualities* ; there are no new affections anfwering thefe new thoughts in our minds ; and this feems to be a more proper way of fpeaking in this cafe : becaufe there is indeed no refemblance between *the primary qualities* and our *ideas* of them, which are the modes of a different fubftance.

§ 19, *page* 116. The *fuperficies* of bodies do for the moft part modify the light that falls upon them, and fo their *colour* feems to be conftant : but it is oftentimes modified before it comes at them, and they reflect it to our eyes with that modification, and then their colour is altered ; and this new colour is as much their colour while they continue in that pofture, as the other colour is at all other times.

CHAP. IX.
Of PERCEPTION.

§ 1, *page* 121. PERCEPTION is the immediate felf-confcioufnefs of ideas in the mind, or of the natural relation of one or more ideas as exifting in and appearing to the underftanding.*

The word *perception* is feldom or never ufed for *thinking in general* ; becaufe thinking comprehends the acts of the *will*, as well as the *underftanding* ; and the *will* was never reckoned among the perceptive faculties, though it has great influence in the improvement of them.†

* Mor. Phil. p: 193. † Ibid. p. 58.

Perception, conception, or apprehenſion is the mere
ſimple contemplation of things offered to our mind,
without affirming or denying any thing concerning
them; the form under which theſe things appear to
the mind, or the reſult of our conception, is called an
idea.*

Perception is that act of the mind whereby it becomes conſcious of any thing, when preſent.†

§ 8, *page* 123, *line* 8. *Of a flat circle variouſly*
ſhadowed.   Becauſe the bottom of the eye being a *ſuper-*
ficies, nothing but a *ſuperficies* can be there painted;
and ſo all the ſolidity and thickneſs of bodies is loſt : ſo
thoſe parts of a globe, which are directly oppoſit. ..
the eye, and ſo on a parallel ſituation to it make the
greateſt image in it, and conſequently the brighteſt and
ſtrongeſt colour; whereas thoſe on either ſide, the further they go towards the tangent lines on the globe,
the leſs images they make in the eye : as a circle, which
was at firſt directly oppoſite and parallel to the eye by
bending any way from it, makes at firſt the image of
an *ellipſis,* and at laſt of a *line* only.

Where any body is more white, or otherwiſe enabled
to reflect the light ſtrongly, the nearer it will appear,
and the leſs luminous the farther off: the reaſon is, becauſe in the natural fabric of the eye, the nerves that are
cauſed to move and thereby defend it againſt the more
preſſing light, contract ſo as it is, and muſt be, to ſee an
object that is very near : ſo that there is no need of
experience to teach us that *ſhade* ſtands for *figure*; for the
parts from which the ſhade comes will, by the ſtructure
of the eye, appear further off than otherwiſe they
would, and ſo the whole ſuperficies of the globe appear
protuberant, as it really is.‡

Page 124, *line* 22. *Or that a protuberant angle.——*
The inequality of the *angles* which preſſed his hand, is

* Watts Log. p. 5.   † Ibid. p. 8.   ‡ Ibid. p. 60.

wholly

image of the eye; a *cube* making nothing but a *parallelogram.*

Quære, Whether he would not by nature know the difference? or in other words, whether there be not conftituted in nature a neceffary connexion between a certain motion upon the organ of touch, and a certain perception, and a certain figure at the bottom of the eye, and the fame perception.*

§ 9, *page* 125, *line* 8. *We bring ourfelves to judge. Sc.* in the inftance he hath given, that the thing we fee is of an uniform colour, though the *idea* we have in our mind, when we fee it, is of a thing *varioufly fhadowed.* We bring ourfelves to judge thus, by our having obferved, that this idea hath been often produced in us by the convex figure of a globe of an *uniform colour.*

§ 14, *page* 127. The inftance here given fmells fo ftrong of a certain principle that man is nothing but an organized body, with the knack of *thinking* tacked to it at certain times, that it may be enough to awaken any one that is concerned for the *immortality of human fouls,* to fee the dangerous confequence of it.†

CHAP. X.

Of RETENTION.

§ 2, *page* 128. *THERE is an ability in the mind, &c.* From hence fome infer *innate* principles, though there be not an actual perception of the feveral parts of thofe propofitions, only a *natural* facility in the mind, to apprehend, connect, or disjoin them, when occafion offers the thoughts of them, juft as there is a *power* in the loadftone to draw iron, before it ac-

* Lee, p. 60.   † Ibid. p. 61.

tually exerts that power, and that is all they mean by *natural* or *innate.**

§ 3, *page* 129. To thefe may be added *method*, by which things, that are a-kin to one another, may be fo placed together in one confideration, as to make our thoughts eafily fucceed one another in train.†

§ 7, *page* 131. I am apt to think it is always *aɛtive*, i. e. that there is an *aɛtion* required in the mind, *diſtinɛt* from the *effeɛt* which the impreffion left.‡ The aɛt of the *memory* is as *diſtinɛt* from that which occafions it, as *fenfation* itfelf, from the *motion* which comes from the objeɛt.§

Memory, as we are aɛtive in it, is the power itfelf belonging to the foul, whereby it applies the perceptive capacity to the confideration of any former objeɛt.

Memory, as we are paffive in it, is only a thing being brought into the perception, with a fecondary or concomitant perception, which diſtinguiſhes it from a new perception, and makes it appear only a perception renewed, or that it was there once at leaſt before.‖

§ 10, *page* 133. In this inftance of birds, there is wanting fomething of convincing evidence that they are *confcious* of what they do. That the finging of fome birds is in a great meafure *mechanical,* is manifeft from their finging more *briſkly* in a room where there is moft walking, talking, or any fort of *noiſy* motion.¶

* Lee, p. 62.   † Ibid.   ‡ Baxt. p. 289.
§ Lee, p. 63.   ‖ Baxt. p. 290.   ¶ Lee, p. 63.

CHAP.

CHAP. XI.

Of Discerning, and other Operations of the Mind.

§ 3, *page* 136, *line* 17. *THAT the same piece of sugar,* &c. It is not true that the mind does at the *same time* perceive those two qualities in the sugar; it is at *different* times, as much as if they had been two different bodies, though they are in the same piece of sugar.*

§ 5, *page* 137, *line* 14. *Belonging to general ideas.*—There are really no *general substances or modes,* and consequently no *ideas* of general things; because there is nothing properly *general* but *words* or *names,* which are applied to *several* things. The reason is, because the mind observes those several things to *agree* to that which is the reason or foundation of that *common* or *general* name. †

§ 7, *page* 137, *line* 7. *Ever compound them,* &c. If they have the *shape* of their master in their *eye,* the *sound* of his voice in their *ears,* &c. one would think they can hardly avoid the having the *image* or *idea* of him in their brains, and that is a *compound idea.*

They appear not to miss them, &c. This has some appearance of an argument, that they do not either perceive or remember; for perceiving or remembering without distinction is not perceiving or remembering at all, or at least of no use. ‡

§ 8, *page* 138. *Names* are not always the *signs* of *ideas.*§ The word *nothing* is the *sign* that our mind

---

* Lee, p. 65.   † Ibid.   ‡ Ibid. p. 66.

§ B. 3, c. 3, § 9.   Proced. of the Und. b. 2, c. 5.   King de Or.
M. p. 7.   Watts Log. p. 1, c. 3, § 3.   Berkley concerning the
Princ. of Hum. Know. Introd. p. 6,   Chamb. Dict. in Abstract,
and general.

conceives a thing as not *exifting*, or of the *negation of exiftence* ; but we have no *idea* of *nothing*, nor of that act of the mind by which we confider a thing as not exifting.＊

Whatever may be denied of abftract ideas, it is certain all true demonftration is in abftract ideas.†

§ 9, *page* 138, *line* 11. Abftraction is certainly a different act of the mind from fenfation, whence reflection and abftracted ideas have their original; though perhaps fenfation and reflection may furnifh us with all the firft objects and occafions whence thefe abftracted ideas are excited and derived. Nor in this fenfe and view of things can I think Mr. Locke himfelf would deny my reprefentation of the original of abftract ideas, nor forbid them to ftand for a diftinct fpecies.‡

The abftract natures of things confift folely in idea, and are not properly objects that can enter by material organs.§

§ 11, *page* 139. There is a gradation or fcale of affent of the principle of action among creatures, in proportion to their perfection. Brutes and men are fpontaneous with regard to the motions of their bodies. But men have further a power of directing arbitrarily their perceptive capacity to and throughout their paft perceptions, which brutes have not, (and therefore cannot be called thinking creatures.)||

And this is the fpecific difference betwixt rational and irrational beings, as this power is the foundation of the rational nature.¶

§ 13, *page* 140, *line* 16. *Hence it comes to pafs, &c.* Hence it is plain that *ideas* are not the foundation of *certainty* or

＊ Lee, p. 66.　† Baxt. N. p. 310.　‡ Watts Log. p. 32.
§ Watts Log. p. 91.　Baxt. p. 84, p. 89, p. 134. Not. p. 86.
|| Baxt. p. 84.　¶ Ibid. p. Not. 79, 84, 107, 156. Brown ou the Underft. p. 173.

true

true knowledge; for if they are, how fhall a *fober* man judge he himfelf is not *mad* ? for mad men's and fober men's *ideas* are equally *true ideas*.*

CHAP. XII.

Of Complex IDEAS.

§ 2, *page* 144. *A* Complex *Idea* is made by joining two or more *fimple ideas* together; but when feveral of thefe ideas of *a different kind* are joined together, which are wont to be confidered as dif-tinct fingle beings, this is called a *compound* or *collective idea.*†

§ 4, *page* 145. The word mode is generally ufed for any property, quality, affection of a fubftance, by which it is either diftinguifhed from other fubftances or from itfelf.‡

A mode is that which cannot fubfift in and of itfelf, but is always efteemed as belonging to, and fubfifting by the help of fome fubftance, which for that reafon is called its fubject.

It is by fome authors applied chiefly to the relations or relative manners of being : but in logical treatifes it is often ufed in a larger fenfe, and extends to all attri-butes whatever, and includes the moft effential and in-ward properties, as well as outward refpects and rela-tions, and reaches to actions themfelves, as well as to manners of action.§

* Baxt. p. 68.   † Watts Log. p. 33.
‡ Watts Log. p. 69.   § Ibid. p. 16.

CHAP. XIII.

Of Simple Modes ; and first, of the Simple Modes of Space.

§ 1, *page* 147, *line* 8. MODIFICATIONS *of the same idea.* The *modifications* of any thing are only the different *modi exiſtendi*, or manners of exiſting belonging to that thing : *that is,* when a thing exiſts in different ſtates or conditions, degrees or quantities, &c. theſe may be called different *modi exiſtendi,* or *modifications* of a thing.

§ 5, *page* 148. *Figure,* in fewer words, is nothing but the determination of *ſpace* or *body.**

§ 12, *page* 153. The idea we have of ſpace is of extenſion in the abſtract, not of a concrete extended ſubſtance.†

The extenſion of body implies a particular action exerted, but the extenſion of ſpace implies no ſuch thing. Space has all the true marks of neceſſary extenſion, matter has all the contrary. To ſay, once ſpace was not extended implies a contradiction : it is impaſſive, without figure, location, diviſion, motion.‡

§ 16, *page* 154. This dilemma is avoidable only by owning *ſpace* to be *ſubſtance* (though not *body,*) neither *material,* nor *cogitative.§*

---

* Watts Log. p. 71.   † Baxt. p. 350. Watts Log. p. 13, 17.
‡ Baxt. p. 351.   § Lee, p. 73.   Carteſ. Princ Phil. p. 2, § 20. Newt. Princ. Math. Schol. Generale ad Fin. ejuſdem Optic. Qu. 20, p. 315.   Dr. Clarke Dem. Prop. 2, his Letters to Leibnitz, p. 1, 11, 41, 55, 77, 101, 125, 181, 299, &c.—Ralphſon de Spa. Reali. c. 5.—Jac. Ode. Princ. Nat. Philoſ. p. 22, 48.—Notes or Or. of Ev. Cudworth, Intell. Syſt. 644, 766.—Green's Prin. Phil. b. 1, c. 4, § 8. 18.—Bayle Dict. p. 2790, 3083.—Colliber's Enquiry into the Being and Attrib. of God.—Gretton a priori, c. 6, 7.—Watts Philoſ. Eſſ. 1, p. 21.

§ 21,

§ 21, *page* 157. The controverſy about a *vacuum* cannot be directly ended; unleſs it could be proved either, that there is no *ſpace*, but where there is ſuch a *body* in it as does produce ſome *ſenſible* effect: or that there is ſome *ſpace*, where there is no *body* that can affect our *ſenſes*; both which are equally impoſſible to be proved.*

Stretch his hand beyond his body? Yes; if there is *ſpace* which is not *body*; but this is begging the queſtion: otherwiſe, I anſwer, No; except there come ſo much *matter* from beyond the confines, as to fill that *ſpace* which the hand left.†

§ 24, *page* 159. This is the beſt argument to prove a *vacuum*, viz. becauſe we can ſo naturally conceive *ſpace* diſtinct from *body*.‡

CHAP. XIV.
Of Duration, and its Simple Modes.

§ 12, *page* 167. THOUGHTS cannot be meaſured in length any more than they can be deſcribed by figures or colours; ſo that meaſuring duration by them ſeems like meaſuring pain by the inch or foot. And therefore we may have ſome notion of duration or time by our conſciouſneſs merely of the ſucceſſion of our thoughts; yet they cannot come near the being a proper ſtandard, or adequate meaſure of it.§

§ 18, *page* 169. Time is defined by Leibnitz, to be the order of ſucceſſion of created beings.‖

* Lee, p. 73. Baxt. p. 37.   † Lee, p. 74.
‡ Lee, p. 75.   § Ibid. p. 78.
‖ Baxt. p. 375. Not. Ult.

§ 31, *page* 178. *External objects* cannot operate upon the mind any otherwise than by *present* impression, and therefore the knowledge or notion we have of *duration, time,* and *eternity,* is gained by the exercise of our *natural faculties* of imagining and reasoning, and not by *sensation* only.*

CHAP. XV.

Of Duration and Expansion considered together.

§ 12, *page* 188. TO these two particulars, wherein space and duration differ, may be added a third, viz. that space is something real, and distinct from the mind conceiving it; but duration is only a mode of the mind's conception concerning the existence of itself, and other things.†

CHAP. XVI.

Of NUMBER.

§ 1, *page* 189. NUMBER, abstracted from the thing numbered, and from the names and figures by which it is expressed, is nothing but a thought or mode of conception, and is improperly called an *idea.*‡

CHAP. XVII.

Of INFINITY.

§ 6, *page* 197, *line* 16. BUT *in other ideas it is not so.*— These words seem to suppose that we can have an idea of the greatest whiteness that can be; but this we can no more have, than

* Lee, p. 81.   † Ibid. p. 84.   ‡ Ibid. p. 89.

of

of the greateſt degree of extenſion that can be. We may indeed ſuppoſe a thing ſo white, that, if adding a greater degree to it, will make a different *idea* in our fancy or imagination; but this he hath alſo obſerved of the addition of ſpace and duration, when the *ideas* under conſideration are very big or ſmall.* But notwithſtanding this, we add to any degrees of *whiteneſs*, ſtill greater degrees of it, which, though leſs or equal will not, will increaſe it *in infinitum*, juſt as the increaſe is made in *extenſion*.

§ 7, *page* 198. Every idea is finite or limited, and therefore to ſay the idea of infinity is limited, is a flat contradiction; and to ſay that it is a continual growing idea, does not mend the matter. A perſon of ſixteen years old is a growing perſon, but the number is not ſo, for that will be immutably the ſame; and the attributing that to the number which is a fixed limited mode of our conception, which is proper only to the thing numbered, creates all the confuſion.†

§ 13, *page* 202. Though we have no complete and adequate idea of infinite, this does not prove that our notion or knowledge of infinity is not poſitive; for we may have a poſitive notion, or rationally grounded knowledge, of that which we do not comprehend.‡

§ 14, *page* 202, *line* 4. *He that conſiders that the end is body.*—This ſeems not a ſufficient anſwer to the argument alledged; for though the end, *i. e.* the extreme parts of any thing be as much parts, and as poſitive beings as the middle parts, yet they may alſo be conſidered, as they are in this argument, *ſc.* as the negation of further *extenſion*. But an anſwer may be fetched from the argument itſelf. For

* B. 2, c. 15, § 9, p. 148.   † Lee, p. 89.
‡ Lee, p. 89. ---Not. on King. ---Cudw. Int. Syſt. p. 647. ---Jac Ode Theol. Nat. p. 27. ---Ralphſon Dem. de Deo, p. 2.

granting what was demanded in the argument, that the *end* of *space* is *nulla extensio ulterior*, an *infinite space* therefore is *quod non habet nullá ulterioré extensionem*; now becaufe we know not how much this *aliqua ulterior extensio* is, which, as he elfewhere expreffes it, is a confufed, incomprehenfible remainder, we cannot have a clear, complete *positive idea* of *infinite space*. We have no *idea* of *infinite space* for this reafon, when I have not the *idea* of all the parts of any thing, I have no perfect *idea* of the whole thing; and fince *infinite space* is made up of infinite parts, *fc.* fuch parts as I can come to no end of, I have not a complete *idea* of *infinite space*; for if I had, I fhould have an *idea* of all the parts of it, and then the mind would come to an end of thofe parts which have no end at all; *which is abfurd.*

§ 15, *page* 204, *line* 2. *This is plain negative*, &c.— What a *negative idea* is, or how part of an *idea* can be faid to be *negative*, is to me unintelligible. I underftand what a *negative proposition* is, as *a horfe is not a ftone*; but I have no *idea* of what is *not a ftone*. But yet I have no *positive* reafon to believe that propofition is very true. A *negative idea* therefore is very obfcure, unlimited, or rather no *idea* at all.*

CHAP. XVIII.

Of the other Simple Modes.

Page 209. **O**F *other fimple modes.*—It is not evident from the defcription here given, whether they be thofe he calls *fimple modes*, or thofe he calls *mixed*; but they feem to be fuch *fimple modes* as are variations of the fame *fimple idea*.

* Lee, p. 100.

CHAP.

CHAP. XIX.

Of the Modes of Thinking.

§ 1, *page* 212. *Of the Modes of thinking.*—The author now ufes the word *mode* again in its ufual fenfe, not that new one he hath made for it.

What this author calls the *modes of thinking* are only the feveral *operations* of the mind according to the *variety* of the objects, or the *manner* of its being employed about them.*

It is as abfurd that the bare reprefentation of things fhould be under the choice and conduct of the underftanding, as it is that we fhould fee what we pleafe only when we look out of our window to the neighbouring fields. The foul reafons full as confiftently as an unexperienced ftranger would do about new and unknown objects.†

§ 4, *page* 214, *line* 11. *The mind fixes itfelf.*—It were to be wifhed that Mr. Locke had applied this to the poffibility of matter's thinking.‡

§ 4, *page* 214. This is fpecious at firft view, but is indeed a very equivocal argument, and concludes different ways according to the different acceptation of the word effence. He grants that thinking is action, and fuppofes effence to be the internal unknown conftitution of things whereon their difcoverable qualities depend. Now that thinking or action, which is a known property of the foul, fhould be the internal, unknown conftitution of the foul is a contradiction, and, proving the contrary, is proving what was never denied. But this is not the genuine acceptation of the word effence. (*Vide infr. p.* 44, § 6.) From whence we

---

* Lee, p. 22.   † Baxt. p. 261.   ‡ Ibid. p. 192.

may fee the fallacy of Mr. Locke's argument. He makes effence the internal, unknown conftitution of things; and becaufe it is contradictory, that thought fhould be of the effence of the foul in this fenfe, he infers it is not of the effence of the foul in the other fenfe, i. e. fo as to be infeparable from it; but that thought is effential to the foul, in the laft fenfe, may be thus proved. It muft be effential to one of the two, fubftances, i. e. either to matter or fpirit; otherwife the higheft perfection in nature muft be merely cafual, or an extraneous accident in the univerfe, but it can nei-ther be effential to matter, nor accidental. (_Vide infr._ _p._ 140.) Ergo, it muft be effential to fpirit, or fuch ɛ property which cannot be feparated from it without deftroying its nature. Or if thinking is effential neither to body or foul, how come we at all to think? Is it by mere accident? If fo, it is poffible the foul fhould never think. If it be faid the foul lays down and takes up thinking at pleafure, (by its own power, &c.) it is a direct contradiction. If the foul pleafes to take up thinking after intermiffion, it muft be previoufly thoughtful: if it be faid to. ftand in need of fome ex-ternal principle to bring back thought to it, this is to own that it would never think again of itfelf, but be a dead inactive fubftance, unlefs reftored by fome exter-nal being. And the argument muft come to this on Mr. Locke's hypothefis, if the foul were for any the leaft time without thought. The power of thinking in a fubftance once dead, cannot be conceived, becaufe it is contradictory. Life itfelf confifts in being perci-pient, in this we are neceffary, and if we are percipient, we muft have perceptions by the terms: thus it is very conceivable, that the foul fhould remit its activity in thinking through all degrees, till at length it can remit no farther, and finds itfelf neceffary in having fome per-ception or other.*

* Baxt. p. 153.

Thinking

Thinking, (allowing it a variable property) may invariably belong to the foul : as figure is a variable property of matter, and yet invariably and infeparably belongs to matter ; and as it is only the exercife of power, not the power itfelf, that is fubject to the variation of being intended or remitted. This does not make the power itfelf feparable from the foul. Again, Mr. Locke himfelf grants that *thinking* is the condition of being awake (*Sup. p.* 72,) a property then capable of being intended or remitted, neceffarily belongs to the foul, at leaft for that time, and if we were always awake, would always and neceffarily belong to it. And fince we cannot ceafe being awake at pleafure, it is not in our power to become unactive at pleafure, or we are neceffarily active. It is the indifpofition of the body which occafions our not being always awake, that hinders our not always exercifing the power of activity, allowing the foul fometime inactive.*

§ 4, *page* 214, *line* 17. *And laſt of all, &c.*—But this is only *experience* of having no memory of confcioufnefs then, which does not infer that we had no confcioufnefs then. When an evidence makes oath that his memory does not ferve him fo far, how much proves he by this ? Nothing furely on either fide. He only owns that the point in controverfy might have been fo, or otherwife, for any thing he can remember.†

Line 30. *Thinking is the action, &c.*—This opinion is not fafe, nor the reafon well-grounded. For when the mind ceafes *thinking*, fo far as we can conceive, it ceafes to be any thing at all ; and fuppofe the *effence* of any fubftance be taken for the *combination* of all the properties and qualities by which that thing is *diftinguiſhed* from another, then I cannot fee, but that the *felf-activity* of the *foul*, which includes both *thinking* and *motion* too, and which diftinguifhes it from *body*

* Baxt. p. 148. † Ibid. p. 71.

and *space*, may not be capable of *degrees*, of being increased or diminished according to the various states and circumstances in which it shall be, for the exercise of that and other *natural* powers.*

CHAP. XX.

Of Modes of Pleasure and Pain.

§ 2, *page* 216. THESE definitions of *good* and *evil* are not *complete*: 1. Because they seem to confound *cause* and *effect*, for we call *effects good* as well as *causes*. 2. They do not keep up the just distinction between *moral* and *physical* good and evil: for if all be called deservedly *good* that procures *pleasure*, then there is no distinction between *real* and *apparent* good. There are some actions *good* or *evil* by an *immutable* constitution of the wise Author of Nature, and do not depend upon the *variable* opinions of men to make them *otherwise*, whatever they may call them.†

Pleasure and pain appear to be mere sensations, rather than proper ideas.‡

CHAP. XXI.

Of Power.

§ 1, *page* 220, *line* 17. THAT *idea* we call *power*. —*Power* no way differs from that we call a *cause*, but that *power* relates to an *effect before*, and cause to an effect *after* it is actually produced. But neither power, cause, or effect, are *ideas*, purely the *names* we give those modes of conceptions which are formed in our minds, upon our observation of the mutual *relation* of substances, and their *operations* upon another §

---

* Lee, p. 94. † Ibid. p.95. ‡ Watts Ess. 52, p. 81. § Lee, p. 95.

§ 8, *page* 224. *Liberty* is not a *power* to do or forbear any action, &c. nor indeed is it any *power* at all.
It is only the defect, the abfence or fufpenfion at leaft of
a *power* in any agent *diftinct* from that which has the
power of preferring or choofing ; and fo it only fignifies
the *extent or mode* of the mind's power we call the *will*,
and not a *diftinct* power itfelf from the *will*.*

The power of *willing* and *underftanding* is proper
fenfe, but the power of liberty or freedom is nonfenfe.
What any one means therefore by liberty of will, is no
more than this, that no agent, neither God, nor angels,
nor any natural caufe whatever, does irrefiftibly impel,
or mechanically force his will to any good action, or re-
ftrain it from any evil ; but that the only reafon of his
preferring a good action to an evil one is from himfelf.†

§ 8, *page* 224, *line* 13. Liberty confifts not only in
acting according to moral motives where they are ; but
in felf-determination by the power of the will, where
circumftances are indifferent ; and that in the Deity
himfelf.‡

§ 8, *page* 224, *line* 13. *So that the idea of liberty.*—
This is nothing elfe but *r power* to execute the *determinations of the will*, and an exemption from external
force for that purpofe. So that this *liberty* doth not at all
refpect the *determinations of the will*, but fuppofes them
to be over before it comes into play. But the general
and moft common notions of *liberty* concern the very
determinations of the will, and the laft refult of our reafon
and judgement ; and in the firft it is required, whether
the mind be *determined* to will by any *external* caufes,
and if it be, it is certainly not *free*. 2dly, Whether
it be *determined* to will by the refult of its own reafon
and judgement, fo that it muft neceffarily will accord-

* Baxt. p. 97. † Ibid. p. 98. ‡ Ibid. p 367.

ing to fuch refult, and if it be fo *determined*, fome think
it is *not* free, others that *it is.**

§ 8, *page* 224. Mr. Locke takes a great deal of
pains to prove that fuch liberty does not belong to the
will; which is very certain, granting his fenfe of liberty
to be the only one, fince by his definition it is evidently
fubfequent to the choice or prefence of mind, and only
relates to the execution of fuch choice by an inferior
faculty. But then, befide this idea of liberty, which is
nothing to the prefent queftion, there is another previous and equally proper one, which regards the very
determination, preference, or direction of the mind itfelf, and may be called its power of determining to do
or forbear any particular action, or of preferring one to
the other; and if freedom can with any propriety of
fpeech be attributed to one of thefe powers, as he has
conftantly attributed it, why may it not, with equal
propriety, be attributed to the other?†

§ 11, *page* 226. In all thefe cafes, as the acts are
not *voluntary*, are not *volitions*, fo nobody pretends to
liberty in them. But where there is *thought* or *volition*,
there is *freedom* or *liberty*, and in no other cafe. *Freedom of mind* therefore is not its *power* to do or forbear
according to its *volition* or preference, but *liberty* from
the *impulfe* and *reftraint* of other caufes diftinct from
itfelf. That is the true meafure of freedom, where that
power in other *agents* operates upon it, there it is a *neceffary* agent, but where that power is wanting or fuf-
pended, there and there only it is *free* ‡

§ 23, *page* 233, *line* 15. *So that.*—If any one fays,
that when the mind either acts or forbears a thing propofed, it has a *power* at the fame time to do neither,

---

* Vide Infr. § 8.   † Law on K. Notes, p. 245.   ‡ Daxt. p. 100.

and therefore that proceeds from its own *free* determination, that it doth either of them at all; this *determination* muſt proceed from an *antecedent* will.

§ 25, *page* 234, *line* 4. *Whether a man be at liberty.*
—This ſeems to be a quibble upon the word *pleaſes,* which had been avoided by ſaying *either of the two;* and the queſtion being ſo worded would have been ſo far from carrying its *abſurdity* ſo manifeſtly in it, that it would have been that great and famous one concerning the *freedom of man's will.*

But what does it ſignify to me that I muſt neceſſarily take one ſide, or the other, right or wrong, ſo long as I can chuſe either of them indifferently? If I can chuſe either· of the two. Here is full room for the exerciſe of liberty, and whether I can or no, ought to have been Mr. Locke's next queſtion; inſtead of which he ſlips in this abſurd query, *Whether a man, &c.**

§ 29, *page* 236. Freedom may be juſtly predicated of the will, or of the mind in exerciſe of it; not indeed his kind of freedom, i. e. that of acting, which belongs to another faculty; but freedom, in our ſenſe of the word, i. e. a certain phyſical indifference, or indeterminateneſs in its own exerciſe, which is what moſt men underſtand by lib. arbitrium. For if there be ſuch a liberty in human nature, we have then got an abſolutely ſelf-moving principle, which does not want any thing out of itſelf to determine it, which has no phyſical connection with, and of no conſequence no occaſion for that grand determiner *anxiety, &c.*

To affirm that the mind or will is determined by the preſent ſatisfaction, uneaſineſs, &c. is ſaying, that it generally has ſome motives from without, according to which it determines the above-mentioned powers; though in reality it always can, and often does the con-

* Vide Bext. p. 90, 116, 119. Strutt's Remarks; p. 38.

trary, *vide* § 30, 46, 53, which no one in his right
fenfes will difpute.*

§ 30, *page* 236.   Mr. Locke feems to put the caufe
after the effect, as he fometimes makes anxiety concomitant, fometimes confequent; and § 31, he fays the one
is fcarce diftinguifhable from the other.   But this fame
defire appears to me to be the very determination of the
will itfelf; what we abfolutely defire we always will, and
v. v. whether it be in our power to purfue that will, and
produce it into act or not; and indeed defire feems no
otherwife diftinguifhable from volition, than as the
latter is generally attended with the power of action,
which the former is confidered without: this is all the
diftinction they are capable, which yet is only nominal;
nor do his inftances prove any real difference.   In the
1ft cafe, here are two oppofite wills, or a weak imperfect volition conquered, by and giving way to a ftronger,
or rather here is but one actual will in the cafe, and
the other is only hypothetical.   2. In this cafe I defire to bear the gout rather than a worfe evil that may
attend the removal of it.   His axiom, therefore, is not
true, that wherever there is pain there is a defire to be
rid of it.

But, in reality, I believe Mr. Locke intends by *defire*
what we mean by *will*, as in § 48 it is called the power
of preferring, and puts volition into the place of action.
§ 16, 28, 30, c. 23, § 18, where he defines the will to
be a power of putting body into motion by thought.
The fame notion runs through all his letters to Lim-
borch.†

§ 31, *page* 237.   Uneafinefs can never determine
the mind to will one action before another, where both
are entirely equal; of which kind numberlefs occur in
life.‡

* Law on K. p. 249, N. 45.   † Ibid. p. 257.   ‡ Ibid. p. 78.

This is but a scanty definition of *desire*; for a man may desire a thing which lies so much in his power to obtain, that it shall give him no *uneasiness* at all. The *uneasiness* men experience in that passion arises and falls as the difficulty, trouble, and hazard of the means of obtaining the thing desired increase or abate; and it may so happen, that the *delight* which the mind proposes to itself in the enjoyment, very often extinguishes all sense of that *uneasiness*; and then nothing is the *motive* to the will but the *proposed good.* *

§ 33, *page* 238. That uneasiness is not only the spring of ill actions, and most of the common actions of life, there is no doubt; but whether it be of *charity*, *piety*, *mercy*, *&c.* or other actions properly *praise-worthy*, which are the grounds and reasons of singular rewards, is much to be questioned. And,

2dly, If that principle be admitted to be the *motive* of the will, whether the minds of men would not be too much humbled, to have all their actions governed by the same principle than those of *brutes* are. And,

3dly, It becomes us to be cautious, that *human nature* be not by that principle debased to that degree as to come too to *mechanism*. For hunger and thirst, and such like natural *uneasinesses*, act upon our bodies, and consequently on our minds, almost as necessarily as weights upon clocks, to make them strike at their due times.

§ 36, *page* 241, *line* 10. *We cannot apprehend.*— These words seem to intimate that this is the effect of reasoning in us, which is not agreeable to experience; the account of this matter might therefore better be deduced from the *wisdom of God* in the contrivance of our nature; for since he designed us for *happiness*, he may

* Law on K. p. 104.

juftly be conceived to make that *determinate* our wills, which removes what is contrary to that.

§ 44, *page* 247. The reafon of men's not govern-ing all their actions by the view of eternal happinefs, and fo in proportion to the true value of the good they aim at, may be as well accounted for from the want of a due confideration of the *nature* and *certainty* of that happinefs, and the diverting, and more prefent plea-fures they meet with, as from the fenfe of a prefent *un-eafinefs*. For as a due confideration of the *nature* and *certainty* of that happinefs raifes the mind to its juft height of *defire* and *preference*; fo the *uneafinefs* that comes from the means only wears off and becomes no, *motive* at all to *good* men.*

§ 47, *page* 249. This act of fufpenfion muft either be founded in the felf-moving power of the mind, and confequently be naturally independent on all motives, reafons, &c. and an inftance of the mind's abfolute freedom from any external determination; which is a contradiction to Mr. Locke's general hypothefis: or elfe it muft be determined, by fome motive or external caufe, and then it will be difficult to make it free in any fenfe.†

Page 249, *line* 12. *In this lies liberty.*—Were we in fuch a ftate of perfection that our *defires* always tended to our *happinefs*, this would be a determination of *liberty*; but fince in the condition we are we fhould oftener defire *wrong* than *right* (*fenfual* pleafures being more apt to be fuggefted to our minds than *rational* ones) our being able to fufpend the execution of our *defires* gives room for thought and reflexion; and the more our *defires* and *volitions* are the refult of them, the more *free* we are; for thofe *actions* are moft *free*, which

* Lee, p. 105.   † Law on K. p. 264, vide § 52.

are from a lively fenfe, and forcible conviction of the *goodnefs* of what we do, though we could not do otherwife, than thofe we have a cold indifference to.

§ 48, *page* 250, *line* 1. *This is fo far from being a reftraint.*—§ 50, *page* 251, *line* 30. *Such determinations abridge not.*—The author (as appears from the inftances he prefently gives) underftands by *freedom*, an exemption from the force of external caufes, which might hinder the execution of our *determination*, if we did determine; not an exemption from the force of our determination, when we make any; for according to thefe we muft act when we do act. Now though it will not be granted him, that he hath fecured the *freedom* of our minds, becaufe his reftraining the word *freedom* to the fenfe he ufes it in will not be allowed, fome underftanding by it an indifferency after the utmoft determinations of the mind; yet it is as eafy to fhew that a neceffary compliance with thefe determinations is no *abridgement of freedom*; for fince the freedom of an action confifts in that lively fenfe and conviction of the goodnefs of it, and that ardor, and impetus, and tendency of the mind to it, with which it is performed; and fince we always act with this difpofition of mind when we act upon the *refult* of our reafons and judgements; though we be neceffitated always to act according to this *refult*, we are neverthelefs *free* in our actions; becaufe they would ftill be performed with that difpofition of mind in which *freedom* confifted; whereas, on the contrary, if we were perfectly indifferent after the utmoft determinations of our minds, if the fenfe and conviction of the goodnefs of an action, the confequent ardour and tendency of the mind to it, did not always carry us to act, it is evident the external caufe fometimes muft do it; and we fhould be liable to. be determined by them, which is a flavery and fubjection to fuch caufes. So that we fee that a *neceffary* compliance with the dictates of our *mind* is not only *confiftent* with *freedom*, but is the main *prefervative* and *fecurity* of it.

§ 48, *page* 250.   Upon the fuppofition of our being inviolably determined in willing by our judgement, it would be really impoffible for us to will amifs or immorally, let our judgements be ever fo erroneous.   The caufes of which, (§ 64, *page* 262, *line* 4) *proceed from the weak and narrow conftitution of our minds*, and are moft of them out of our power; either therefore we can will without and againft a prefent judgement, and therefore are not neceffarily (*i. e.* phyfically) determined by it, or we cannot be guilty of a wrong volition, whatever proves the one by neceffary confequence eftablifhes the other.   Farther, there are innumerable indifferent actions which occur daily, both with refpect to abfolute choofing and refufing, or to choofing among things abfolutely equal, equal both in themfelves and to the mind, on which we evidently pafs no manner of judgement, and confequently cannot be faid to follow its determination in them.*

§ 52, *page* 253, *line* 15.   *Whatever neceffity, &c.*— If this force which draws us towards happinefs in general, be abfolute and irrefiftible, as his words import, it will draw us equally towards all particular appearances of it, and confequently prove as bad a ground for fufpenfion as for liberty.   But in truth this fufpenfion is neither founded in any neceffity of purfuing happinefs in general, nor in itfelf an original power of the mind diftinct from that of volition, but only one particular exercife or modification of it.

§ 58, *page* 258, *line* 7.   *A man never chufes amifs.*— This expreffion is of the fame nature with thofe that follow: fc. *we fhould undoubtedly never err in the choice*

* Law on K. p. 251.

ef

of good, we should infallibly prefer the best.—The reason of them is this, because he suppoſes that when all *future* conſequences of our actions were removed, thoſe that had the moſt *preſent* happineſs, would be really the beſt for us, would be for our *true good.*

Ibid. He knows what beſt pleaſes.—He would always chuſe the greateſt *preſent* good, if no *future* conſequences attended his choice.

Ibid, line 8. *Things in their preſent enjoyment—The apparent and real good—The preſent good and evil.*—Theſe expreſſions are all of the ſame nature, and import this much : That theſe things which are concluded with the *preſent* enjoyment, and have no *future* conſequences, are truly and really ſo *good* as they ſeem to be ; ſc. as they are at *preſent*, and no better : they have juſt ſo much good as they bring along with them, and no more : whereas others, upon account of their future conſequences, may be either better or worſe, may really have either more or leſs *goodneſs* than they *ſeem* to have, ſc. than they bring along with them at *preſent.* Such, therefore, in the main, all circumſtances taken in, may be different from what they ſeem, may have more or leſs *true* and *real* good, if their conſequences be conſidered, than is *apparently preſent.*

Ibid. line 16. *Were the pains of honeſt induſtry.*—There is ſo great difference betwixt theſe two *pains*, that we ſhould certainly chuſe the former ; as alſo betwixt the two *pleaſures* mentioned, that we ſhould certainly chuſe the latter. Theſe inſtances therefore are brought to prove the aſſertion above, *that we ſhould chuſe* the greateſt *preſent* good, if no *future* conſequences attended the choice.*

§ 59, *page* 259, *line* 7. *Our deſires look beyond—and carry the mind—according to the neceſſity.*—Sc. never but

---

* Vide Mor. Phil. p. 195.

when we think that abfent good neceffary to our happinefs, and that is not often.

§ 63, *page* 262, *line* 49. *For that lies not in compar-*
ing.—For here it is fuppofed there is none to compare.
Ibid. line 51. *But in another fort of wrong judgement,*
which is.—Concerning things confidered, as they may
prove *good* or *evil* to us hereafter: this fort of *wrong*
judgement is defcribed § 66, *poge* 264, and it differs
in this from the former, that, in that, *prefent and*
future pleafure or pain were confidered fimply in themfelves, *abftracted* from the things which procured them;
but this begins with the *things* themfelves, and
confiders whether they will procure any *future good* or
evil, and how much.

§ 68, *page* 265, *line* 18. *And very often in the means*
to it.—When we have hit upon fome means that we
like, we take up with them, and think not any other
neceffary, though perhaps they are.
Ibid. line 27. *That they do not eafily.*—If thefe be
meant of the miftake of the means, the fenfe is, that
we more eafily take up with the means we have lighted
upon, when others feem unpleafant. For this will con-
duce to make us think them unneceffary; if they be
underftood of the miftake of the end, the meaning is,
that we can hardly think that any part of our happinefs
which cannot be obtained but by making us unhappy.*

§ 69, *page* 266. It is objected by Leibnitz, That
if the mind could create pleafure by an arbitrary determination and bare election, it might, for the fame reafon produce happinefs in infinitum. But it is furely
no good confequence to infer, that becaufe I can will a
thing abfolutely and freely, therefore I can will it in

* Vide Law on K. p. 333.

infinitum?

infinitum ? May I not as juftly be faid to underftand a thing in infinitum, becaufe I perceive or underftand it at all?*

§ 71, *page* 270, *line* 38. *I wifh they, &c.*—It is antecedent to and independent on any particular thought or judgement, and continues equally independent after them. It remains in the fame ftate after the determination of the judgement, as that Mr. Locke fuppofes of the operative powers of the determination of the will.†

This indifference of the operative powers is what can never conftitute morality, fince their operations are no farther moral than as they are confequent upon, and under the direction of the will.

There muft then be another indifference prior to them, in order to make the exertion of them free in any tolerable fenfe.‡

§ 73, *page* 273. To thefe might be added pofition or diftance ; for it is manifeft, that as the fame body is in different poftures and diftances, it may produce differing perceptions, as of colours, magnitude, figure, &c.

C H A P. XXII.

Of Mixed Modes.

§ 2, *page* 275, *line* 29. *S*EVERAL *of thofe complex ideas.*—Some actions, for inftance, enjoined by law muft have been in the lawgiver's mind before they actually exifted amongft men, becaufe they were performed purfuant to the law, and in obedience to it.

§ 5, *page* 277, *line* 7. *He fhall find the reafon of it to be.*—Sc. it was done for the fame reafon and end that

---

* Law on K. Note, p. 50.   † Ibid. p. 49.   ‡ Vide Sup.

language was inſtituted for.   This collection of ideas
and language had both the ſame end and reaſon.

§ 10, *page* 280.   Some men think *number* has been
as much *modified*, or at leaſt as capable of being ſo, and
having diſtinct names too as *motion* or *thinking*.   But
as for *power* they never ſaw any *modifications* of that but
only of the ſeveral *qualities* or *properties* which give that
name to ſubſtances.*

§ 11, *page* 281, *line* 22.   *And therefore* many words.
—He ſeems to ſuppoſe that creation and freezing are
actions of a different kind from either thinking or motion, and conſequently as we have no idea of.   But
why may not creation be conceived to be a thought in
the divine mind, and volition of God, upon which the
exiſtence of things is neceſſarily conſequent ?   As for
freezing, it is only the ſtopping or diminiſhing the agi-
tation of the parts of water, which is a *modification* of
motion.

CHAP. XXIII.
Of our Complex Ideas of Subſtances.

§ 2, *page* 283.   THE name of *ſubſtance* we give to
any thing whoſe exiſtence we con-
ceive *independent* upon every thing elſe, and in which
ſeveral properties or qualities are united or combined.
And the *nature* and *eſſence* of every particular thing can
be that only by which it is *diſtinguiſhed* from every
thing elſe; the *nature* or *eſſence* of every *ſubſtance* as
diſtinguiſhable from every *quality* is, that its manner of
exiſtence is *independent*, and that it has ſeveral qualities
united in it; and the *nature* and *eſſence* of every *quality*,
as diſtinguiſhable from every *ſubſtance*, is, that its *manner*

* Lee, p. 109.

of exiſtence is dependent, and that it has no *qualities* united in it. And in this ſenſe we have as clear a notion of *ſubſtance* in *general,* or of any *particular ſubſtance,* as we have of *quality in general,* or any *particular* quality. And therefore it is not fair, firſt to require us to abſtract every *property* and *quality* which conſtitutes the *eſſence* or *nature* of it, and then aſk us, *What it is ?* there being no ſuch *ſubſtance* in the whole world.*

§ 5, *page* 290, *line* 14. *The one being ſuppoſed—and the other* ſuppoſed—whatever therefore *be the ſecret.*— The author by theſe expreſſions declares, that there is ſomething to be conſidered in things beſides the *collections* and *combinations* of their *qualities,* ſomething that is the *cauſe* of their conſtant union and perpetual *co-exiſtence,* which is the *ſubſtratum* and *ſupport* of them, which notwithſtanding is utterly unknown to us, and might give occaſion to the old philoſophers to ſay the *eſſences* of things were unknown ; and this indeed ſeems neceſſary to be allowed ; for otherwiſe, of *created ſubſtances,* for inſtance, it muſt be affirmed that God created only ſo many *collections* of *qualities,* which would be harſh and abſurd to ſay.

That we have as good proof of its exiſtence as we have for that of matter, I grant, but to ſay our ideas of their modes and properties are equally clear and diſtinct, appears to be a very groundleſs aſſertion.†

§ 9, *page* 295. *Primary* properties do not conſtitute *complex ideas,* becauſe they are rarely known, for though we can by our ſenſes diſcover, indeed, that in the general there are ſuch *qualities* as *motion, figure, &c.* yet they go not towards making up the *ideas* of particular *bodies,* where we do not perceive them.‡

* Lee, p. 111.
† Brown's Anſwer to Chriſtianity not Myſterious, p. 55
‡ Lee, p. 112.

· ·§ 17, 18. *page* 301. He has before afcribed motivity, or a power of putting body into motion by thought, to fpirit, as one of the *ideas* peculiar to it ; fo that by mobility he feems to mean a capacity in fpirit of being moved by fomething ab extra, and not the power of moving, which is included in motivity, efpecially fince he makes mobility common to both matter and fpirit, which, with fubmiffion, I think is wrong, and tends to. confound the fubftances he would diftinguifh.—A fubftance that no way impedes motion, but effects it, can with no propriety, I think, have the capacity of mobility afcribed to it, as it is to body, a fubftance which refifts motion, and no way effects it, and therefore wants an external mover. To make fpirit material, and fo at once both to caufe and hinder motion, is a plain contradiction. Spirit, it is true, ftops motion, but it is by the fame living efficacy, by which it begins it ; not by a deadnefs or refiftance in itfelf to be moved. Befides, a fpirit when it moves, hath no moment as body hath, proceeding from its vis inertiæ. It cannot be faid to refift, being brought from motion to reft, or v. v. fince it effects thefe changes. If it moved circularly, it could have no centrifugal force. When a man walks his fpirit moves his body, but is not moved by it. If both were moved, there would be no mover. Nay, in the journey betwixt London and Oxford, where the man's fpirit is not the mover, but the horfes move the coach, his body and all, his fpirit does not impede the motion, or make the draught heavier, or is not properly amoved. So that in effect, mobility doth not belong in common both to body and fpirit. Nor, farther, can motion belong to both, but in very different fenfes.

§ 19, *page* 301, *line* 3. *For having, &c.*—It is true. fpirits change place, and motion, in this fenfe, is competent to all finite fpirits. But in this motion they are not moved but movers ; which is the diftinction endeavoured to be confounded. Sceptical people conclude

from this, that whatever moves is material ; but it will
not follow that whatever moves as a mover is material,
and has the relation of matter. For in the idea of the
motion of body, a moved, and not a mover, is implied ;
and the affections of movement, refiftance, and tendency
to move in the fame uniform direction, are neceffarily
included. Were there but one body in the univerfe,
thefe affections would infeparably attend its motion :
and yet then the relation of diftance would never fhew
motion. The diftinction of *ubi* and *loco*, which Mr.
Locke obferves § 21, *page* 302, to be of little ufe to
our conception, was introduced probably to fignify that
body and fpirit occupy fpace after a different manner,
though we cannot conceive that difference of manner.*

§ 23, *page* 303, *line* 6. *If he fays, he knows not what
he thinks.*—The author feems to confound *cohæfion* of
parts with *extenfion*, which are very different *ideas*, and
may be diftinct and feparate in the mind ; for we may
conceive the parts of matter *unam extra aliam*, one being
not in the place where the other is, without any *idea* of
cohæfion, i. e. mutually touching one another at prefent,
but indifferent as to their continuing fo, or being feparated ; we may have therefore a clear *idea* of the *extenfion* of the parts of matter without any *idea* of their *cohæfion*, much more without confidering the *caufe* of
their *cohæfion*. (The beft modern philofophers affirm
it to be done by the conftant *action* of fome immaterial
being, and moft probably of *God* himfelf, who being
every where is the moft able to effect in this in every
part of the univerfe) which is indeed an infupportable
difficulty, but comes not in very properly or very per-
tinently in this place. The truth of this matter is, that
there feems not to be any *difficulty* or obfcurity at all in
either of the *ideas* of *extenfion* and *thinking*, and it is very
improper to inquire into the *manner* or *modes* of them,

* Baxt. p. 48.

which is not different from the things themselves; for as we have a clear *conception* of *extension*, when we reflect upon the matter being in different places, and no two of them in one and the same ; so we have of *thinking*, by reflecting upon the operations of the mind, and to seek any further for the manner, is to seek we know not what.

§ 37, *page* 312. All ideas or notions of *substances* seem to enter into the mind *complicated*, and not *single*, and after they are there, are considered *abstractedly*, and compared, in order to *general* knowledge.[*]

C H A P. XXIV.

Of Collective Ideas *of Substances.*

§ 2, *page* 314, *line* 3. *AND uniting severally.*—These words are but an explication of power of *composition*, and must not be so read or connected with the former as to imply that *collective ideas* of substances can be made by *uniting substances*, which are all *complex ideas.*

In the forming conceptions of single substances, the mind considers those properties and qualities united, as it finds them united, and then by its abstracting power on occasion considers them separated. But in these collective notions the mind compounds the substances, or considers them united, which were in nature separated : The first is called analytical, the other synthetical method by old logicians.[†]

---

* Lee, p. 116.   † Ibid.

CHAP. XXV.

Of RELATION.

§ 8, *page* 319, *line* 28. *AND thofe being all either.—* &c. all *ideas* in general are *fimple* or *complex* : not that the *ideas* of *relation* here treated of can ever be *fimple ones*, for he hath before made them a fpecies of *complex ones*.

CHAP. XXVI.

Of Caufe and Effect, and other Relations.

§ 1, *page* 321. *CAUSE* and *effect* are only the names of *fubftances* given them for *active* or *paffive* qualities in one or the other. The *final* caufe, being only in *intelligent* agents, cannot be any thing more than *modally* diftinct from the *efficient* (as *action* from *agent*). The *material* caufe, being only in *corpo-real* fubftances, cannot be any thing diftinct from the *effect*; nor the formal from the *efficient effect*, being the combination of thofe properties or qualities in the *active* fubftance to operate, or the *paffive* fubftance to receive any new modification. For inftance, in a watch, the conveniencies of knowing the hour, &c. defigned by an artift is the *final* caufe ; the brafs, filver, &c. is the *material* caufe ; the powers and qualities exercifed by the artift denominate him the *efficient*; and the new modification fuperinduced in the materials, when fitly put together, are its *formal* caufe.*

* Lee, p. 118.

CHAP. XXVII.

Of Identity and Diversity.

§ 3, page 327. MERE *exiſtence* is not the *Principium Individuationis*. To judge whether a thing be the *ſame* with itſelf at different times, a man muſt have ſome conception of what that is at one time, that he may compare it with itſelf at another : but that he cannot poſſibly have, that has no *object* for his thoughts, but bare *exiſtence*. The *Prin. Ind.* therefore in any body is its figure, poſition, bulk, motion, or reſt of all its particles, and not its bare exiſtence. The ſuppoſition here made of an *immutable* atom is not only impoſſible, but ſuppoſes that every thing it was to prove, for if it be *immutable*, it muſt be the *ſame*, without all queſtion.

What is the *Principium Ind.* ? Or what is it that makes any one thing the ſame as it was ſome time before ? This is too large and laborious an inquiry to dwell upon here, yet I cannot forbear mentioning this hint, viz. ſince our own bodies muſt riſe at the laſt day, &c. there may be perhaps ſome *original fibres* of each human body, ſome ſtamina vitæ or primæval ſeeds of life, which may have remained unchanged through all the ſtages of life, death, and the grave ; theſe may become the ſprings and principles of a reſurrection and ſufficient to denominate it the *ſame body*. But if there be any ſuch conſtant and vital atoms which diſtinguiſh every human body, they are known to God only.*

§ 4, page 328. The *continual ſucceſſive*, though *inſenſible*, appoſition and union of new particles of the ſame contexture and configuration, helped by the *ſolar* and *central* heat, is ſufficient for plants being called the *ſame*,

---

* Watts Log. p. 111.

young

young and old, without a *common principle* of life, as well as it does of *minerals*.

§ 5, *page* 328. The fuppofition is here again impoffible; for though the comparing *animals* to *machines* be a good fimilitude, as that of filly men to affes, yet it is no proof of its poffibility. *Animal*, therefore, may more properly be faid to be the *fame* by having its parts *united* to the *fame* inward *principle* or caufe of life.*

§ 6, *page* 329, *line* 3. *Nothing but a participation.*—
This participation of the fame continued life may be called the *animal identity*, but it is not in this alone that the *identity of man* confifts, but in this and the *identity* of the foul joined together : fo that if either of thefe two identities be wanting, the *identity of man* is loft; ex. gr. If the *fame* foul fhould fucceffively inform thofe we call the *bodies* of *Seth, Ifmael, &c.* they would all be the fame man, for want of the animal identity ; and if thofe we call the fouls of *Seth, Ifmael, &c.* fhould fucceffively inform any one body, they would not be the *fame* man for want of the *identity* of the foul.

The *identity* of man confifts fomething more than matter organized in the fame manner, in the fame principle of *intellectual* actions, or in the fame individual fpirit united to the *fame* body, however the feveral parts of that body may have infenfibly *changed* in the feveral fucceffive moments and ftates of life. And this we find certain in matter of fact ; but we never yet heard of one foul being united to two complete bodies of human fhape. The fuppofition therefore of its *poffibility* muft be looked upon as fictitious and very unphilofophical. Since God has neither given us any evidence to believe it is fo, by what he has done, nor revealed to us he ever will ; and we have no meafure of poffibility but that.†

---

* Watts Log. p. 122.   † Lee, p. 124.

§ 8, *page* 330.   Inferences grounded on such suppositions as these of the cat and parrot, are mere romance.*

§ 9, *page* 333, *line* 20.   *And as far as this* consciousness.—The meaning of this, and some following expressions of this nature, is not *that personal identity* that reaches no further than the *memory* of our past actions: for we may have perfectly forgot some of them, which yet certainly were the *actions* of our *very selves.*   That which is here asserted therefore is, that supposing any past *actions* return to our minds, either by the power of *remembrance*, or external suggestion, if we have the same *consciousness* of them that we had of them at *first*, and which we have of *present* actions, we are the *same* persons that did them, and not otherwise.

§ 10, *page* 333.   Consciousness is only the repeated and successive acts of the mind, by which it takes notice of its former and successive actions; but actions cannot unite themselves, and therefore that which must make these distinct and successive acts of consciousness to be the actions of one being, must be something distinct from the actions themselves, and that must and can be only the mind itself.   Ergo, it is that and not consciousness that denominates the person the same with himself at different times.†

Page 334, *line* 27.   *Different substances.*—The author's method seems not to be good here; for in this place he takes that for granted, which a little lower in these words, " *Or can be continued in a succession*," he speaks doubtfully of, and § 12, *page* 335, debates as a question.

Ibid. line 29.   *As different* bodies, by the same life.—Sc. *Different particles* of matter falling as fast as they come, into the disposition, or organization that some

---

* Lee, p. 124.   † Ibid. p. 125.

one

ene original mafs had, are ftill efteemed the *fame* vegetable or animal body.

Ibid. line 36. For as far as any intelligent being.—
He feems to fuppofe there may be an intelligent being
(meaning, I believe, his perfon) fubfifting of itfelf, independent of all thinking fubftances, which one after
another may be joined to it; a ftrange thought.*

Ibid. line 48. The fame confcioufnefs uniting.—He
fuppofes two fubftances, one which hath the fame confcioufnefs of the other's paft actions that it hath of its
own prefent ones, to be the fame perfon.

§ 11, *page 335, line 7. Are a part* of ourfelves, &c.
—and fubftance whereof perfonal felf confifted.—The
author feems to have forgot his definitions of perfon
§ 9, *page 333, a thinking intelligent being,* of which certainly matter cannot be a part, and indeed this is not at
all a fit inftance, nor does it come up to the matter in
hand, though he ufes it feveral times afterwards.

The limb, whilft it is vitally united to the body, was
no more a part of our *confcious* felves, than our blood
is. No part, nor indeed the whole body, is any more
than the foul's inftruments in its operations, does not
think, is not confcious of any of its actions. The eye
does not fee, nor the ear hear, &c.—This then feems
rather an argument to prove, that *animus cujufq. eft is
quifq.* becaufe the man is the fame after the limb is cut
off, then the contrary.†

§ 12, *page 335, line 1. And to this* I anfwer.—This
paragraph feems very obfcure, and confufed, and little
or nothing to the purpofe.

Ibid. line 6. It is plain.—They feem to make it the
fame with *animal identity.*

Ibid. line 10. Before they can come to deal with
thefe men.—For thefe men making *animal* and *perfonal*

* Vide § 25.   † Lee, p. 128.

identity the *same*, will demand first of all, as previous and preparatory to all further disputes, why those that allow *animal identity* to be preserved in the *change* of *substances*, will not grant that *personal identity* may also be so preserved : and this the other side must resolve before they enter into any further debates, unless they will deny *animal identity* to be preserved in the change of material *substances*; sc. unless they will, it is one immaterial spirit in brutes, that makes in them the same life.

§ 12, *page* 335. To the two parts of this question may be given these two plain answers : to the first, that if the *thinking substance*, the principle of intellectual operations, be changed, it cannot be the same person. To the second, that if it be not changed, it is the same person.

Ibid. page 335. *A purely material, animal constitution.* —If the fleeting animal spirits be the *soul*, the intelligent being, there will be as many persons as there are distinct animal spirits, or particles of *refined* matter ; for they never make each other conscious of their several motions and actions.

Ibid. page 335. *As well as animal identity.*—But not so much as animal identity is preserved in the change of material substances, except that change be gradual, and insensibly successive in the course of nature.*

§ 13, *page* 336. *That cannot be resolved, &c.*—The two conditions here proposed, are somewhat unreasonable : for 1st, I presume nobody knows what kind of substances those are which *think*; because, if *thinking* of all sort be abstracted, there remains nothing in an intelligent being which we can conceive, and because there is no such sort of substance in the world. 2dly, If *consciousness* be only a power, or *repeated* acts of *knowing*, I ask, whether it can be conceived without a *substance* or something, call it soul or body, wherein that power

* Lee, p. 125.

i2,

is, or of which that *confcioufnefs* is the fucceffive and repeated *action*? 2. Whether men can be *confcious* of
that which they never did, or judge they did that of
which they never thought of doing? And 3, Whether
thought can be imagined without a *fubftance*, any more
than *motion* or *figure* without a body *moving* or *figured*?
And if it be fo, which feems to be the fenfe of all the
world, then *confcioufnefs* neither can conftitute the *perfon*,
nor can be *transferred* from one foul to another, any
more than one man's pain in his head or foot can be
transferred to another's.*

Ibid. line 16. *Will be hard.*—To make this fenfe
run clear thefe words muft be read together : *till we
know what kind of action it is, and how performed in
thinking fubftances*; and the intermediate ones left out.

Ibid. page 16. *What kind* of action.—Sc. What
kind of action this reprefentation of things to our
mind as done by us, which never were really done, is.

Ibid. page 17. *That* cannot be done, &c.—This
fentence, and that which follows, *Who cannot, &c.* are
put in to fhew that if there be fuch a reprefentation of
things to our minds, as is mentioned above, there muft
be alfo a *confcioufnefs* of them.

Ibid. line 20. *The fame confcioufnefs.*—Sc. not being
meant of the individual *confcioufnefs*, for that no one
fubftance can have at different times, but a *confcioufnefs*
of the fame fort or kind.

Ibid. line 26. *As well as feveral reprefentations in
dreams.*—It is true, a man may be deceived at prefent
in a dream, but I never heard that any man ever
dreamed, that he did that which at the fame time he
thought another perfon did, or that he thought, i. e.
was *confcious* of that which he did not think he did, and
fo he was not deceived in the confcioufnefs of the re-
flex act.

* Lee, p. 126.

Ibid. line 35. *How far this.*—He intimates that if thinking be placed in such a system, the *consciousness* of past actions may be transferred from one *thinking* substance to another. (For *animal and personal identity* being then the *same,* preserved in a change of *material* substance, if any one person be the *same* with himself at different times, different substances must be *conscious* of the *same* actions as done by themselves.) And he leaves it to be considered therefore how far the *goodness of God* may be an *argument* against such an *hypothesis* of *thinking.*

§ 14, *page* 337, *line* 2. *Whether* the same.—Whether the same *immaterial being* which alone is *conscious* of the actions of its past duration, may be wholly stript of all such *consciousness.*

Ibid. line 18. *Not having continued.*—Or inactivity, but having been conscious of something or other in every one of those ages.

Ibid. But till he have some of that *consciousness,* which it is impossible to have, it is as impossible for one soul to be in several bodies in different ages, as for two persons, who co-exist, to feel each other's pains or pleasures.*

§ 15, *page* 338. But if there was not the same *soul,* the same principle of intellectual operations, though possibly there might be a new *creation,* there could be no resurrection. It is better therefore to content ourselves with the assurance of a *resurrection,* from reason and revelation, than please ourselves with an *imaginary* and *miraculous* creation.†

§ 18, *page* 340, *line* 16. *Or could own.*—Nor could the finger own any of the actions of the body after the

* Lee, p. 128.   † Ibid. p. 129.

separation;

feparation; for he now fuppofes it to act after the feparation, becaufe it has life.

Ibid. There is no manner of doubt, but that every diftinct foul fhall in the future ftate be made confcious of its good or ill actions, but the grand queftion is, Whether this be poffible, if the foul was annihilated? It is an idle thing to hope for that which almighty wifdom has given us no fort of evidence, that it is fo much as poffible, any more than he has, that all the foul, all its fenfations, and other operations, can be epitomized in a finger.*

§ 21, *page* 342, *line* 2. *Cannot* be the fame man.— Yes; by the *fame* foul being united to *thofe* particles of matter, which compofed his body, when he died, put again into the fame organization or *animal life* at the refurrection: and though fome *new* particles fhould be taken in alfo to complete the work, yet fo long as the old ones were the rudiments, and foundations of it, this would not deftroy *animal identity* according to his own principles.

§ 25, *page* 344, *line* 40. *Any fubftance* vitally united.—Sc. any fubftance whatever in any nature.— But this is a ftrange expreffion, which feems to imply that when any one fpirit is no longer a *man's felf*, by being ftript of its *confcioufnefs*, there ftill remains a *prefent thinking being*, to which a *new fpirit may be vitally united.* And indeed the author has been forced to ufe fome harfh and uncouth ways of fpeaking, by reafon of the ftrangenefs of his notion, in which he feems after all to be miftaken; for it is much more agreeable to reafon that *thinking fubftance and perfon* fhould be *one* and the *fame* thing. It is an extravagant fancy to imagine that *one fpirit* fhould become *confcious* of the actions of *another*, as if they were its own, and fo they *two* be *one*

* Lee, p. 128.

perſon. Nor is the other ſuppoſal much better, that any one ſpirit by loſing the *conſciouſneſs* of all his *paſt* actions, and getting the *conſciouſneſs* of *new* ones, ſhould thereby become *two* perſons. It would not indeed be concerned, as he ſays, in thoſe actions which he had loſt all *conſciouſneſs* of; he would not attribute them to *himſelf*, or think them his *own*; but he would ſtill be the *perſon*, that did them. What the author aſſerts, that *ſuch a ſpirit would not be accountable*; ſc. rewardable or puniſhable for ſuch actions ſeems juſtly queſtionable; he himſelf hath given an inſtance to the contrary among men. And though perhaps it may ſeem moſt probable and agreeable to the divine juſtice and wiſdom, that ſhould men be *conſcious* of what they are rewarded or puniſhed for by him; yet this is by no means certain, at leaſt, as to all *particular* good and bad actions. And I ſuppoſe our author himſelf would ſcruple to allow that an *intellectual ſubſtance*, which according to his own ſuppoſition § 13, *page* 336, had got a *conſciouſneſs* of all other actions, ſhould be *rewardable* or *puniſhable* for them.

CHAP. XXVIII.

Other RELATIONS.

§ 10, *page* 372. *VIRTUE* and *vice* are not mere *arbitrary* names, but reſolvable into *immutable* relations, i. e. are as *immutable* as the ſureſt maxims of *truth* and *falſehood*.*

§ 11, *page* 373. Nothing more is intended by theſe expreſſions, but that virtue was ſo agreeable to the natural ſenſe of mankind that they reckoned praiſe the general reward of it, not *virtue* itſelf. Cic. Tuſc. l. 4. *Virtus eſt affectio animi conſtans convenienſque laudabiles efficiens eos in quibus eſt, ſeparata etiam utilitate laudabiles.*

* Lee, p. 133.

CHAP.

CHAP. XXIX.

Of Clear and Obscure, Distinct and Confused Ideas.

§ 2, *page* 383, *line* 11. *O*UR *simple ideas are clear.—*
He means that then they
are *clear*, when they are such that nature designed we
should have.

Ibid. line 23. *And* the number and order.—For if
there are complex ideas, which are continually varying
as to their number, and order of their ingredients, they
can never be *clear* in the sense above-mentioned.

§ 4, *page* 384, *line* 1. *As a clear idea is that.—*The
perception the mind hath of *clear ideas* is all it can, or
is to have, and is a vigorous, lively perception:

§ 5, *page* 384, *line* 9. *No idea therefore.—*Every
idea considered in itself as in the mind is distinguishable
from all others (different perceptions making it so)
and is only a *confused idea* of the things the names it is
expressed by stand for. Thus the *idea* of a spotted
beast considered in itself is distinct from that of a beast
without spots, and from all other *ideas* in the mind, and
is only a *confused idea* of those beasts expressed by the
names *leopard, lynx, panther.*

§ 8, *page* 386, *line* 12. *This draught.—*These sur-
prizing pieces of art are said to have been invented,
much improved by one Mr. *Matthews*, Fellow of Sid-
ney College, *Cambridge.*

CHAP. XXX.

Of Real and Fantaflical Ideas.

§ 4, *page* 395. BUT moft men think they could have no notions of any *moral virtues or vices* without deriving them from *real* actions either in their own minds, or from the fenfible actions of others; and as every man's notions agree, more or lefs, with that which is founded in nature, fo they are more or lefs perfect, but not more or lefs *real*. And no ideas feem to be *archetypes* or *originals* : they are all, when in the mind, types or copies derived from *real* actions in nature; elfe *virtue and vice* would be arbitrary notions, made according to every man's pleafure and fancy.*

CHAP. XXXI.

Of Adequate and Inadequate Ideas.

§ 2, *page* 397, *line* 1. SIMPLE ideas are *inadequate* as well as *complex* : 1. Becaufe there is no *natural* connexion between thofe *qualities,* when confidered in the *object*, and the *effect* of them, when confidered as in the *mind*; the *effect* is widely different and *incommenfurate* by the caufe. 2. Becaufe we have more knowledge of all the forts of *fingle qualities or modes* of *particular fubftances,* than we could derive from the things confidered in themfelves: fo vaftly do the effects exceed their *original fimple caufes.*

§ 6, *page* 400. The word *effence* is generally ufed for that only by which a thing is *diftinguifhed* from every thing elfe, and in this fenfe we may have as *adequate idea* of any *fubftance* as of any *quality* in it.†

* Lee, p. 136.   † Ibid. p. 138.

Ibid

2

Ibid. line 3. Now those ideas.—In order to under-
stand the author's sense of this matter we must recollect
from what has gone before, what *ideas* we have of *substances,* and how far they answer their *archetypes.*

1. Therefore to begin with the general division of
substance, of matter and spirit, which are all the sorts of
it we know of. The *idea* we have in general of matter
is an *idea* of *solidity, extension, figure, &c.* with an *unknown substratum,* support, or cause of union of these
qualities. The *idea* we have of *spirit* in general is an
idea of consciousness or *thinking* in general with an *unknown substratum* or support also. This *substratum* or
cause of union is the same thing which the men he here
hath to do with, call *real essence, specific essence,* or *internal constitution, &c.* from which all the qualities flow,
upon which they depend, and with which they have a
necessary connexion.

2. The *idea* we have of particular material substances, sc. inanimate, vegetable, animal bodies, consists,
1st, Of all that was in the former idea, because they are
so many parcels of matter. 2dly, Of the supposition
of a division into minute parts, and of a particular
bulk, figure, and motion of those parts, which are
called the *primary qualities* of bodies; which, though
they must needs be supposed, or else all parcels of
matter would be alike, are as unknown to us as the
substratum above. 3dly, Of active and passive powers
discoverable by our senses, which are called secondary
qualities, because they result from the primary ones,
and are indeed all that we think, have ideas of, or conceive in them. So likewise our *idea* of particular *immaterial* substances, sc. God, *angels, human souls,* consists
of the *idea* abovementioned, and the supposition of any
particular *modes* of *thinking* unknown to us, and the
active and passive *powers* we know in them.

Of any of these particular *material* substances (for of
these alone the author treats) sc. *gold,* it may be said,
that its *primary qualities* (sc. the particular *bulk, figure,*

motion, &c. of its parts) are its *real effence*; they are that which diftinguifh it from all other matter in the world, and from whence all its active and paffive _powers_, difcoverable by our fenfes, flow.

From hence it is evident; ıft, In our idea of any particular *material* fubftance, fc. *gold:* the fubftratum of its folidity and extenfion, as it is matter; its *primary qualities*, or real effence, as it is gold : and many of its active and paffive powers, or *fecondary qualities* being unknown; no fuch *idea* can be *adequate*; for fo much as is unknown, it cannot include, reprefent, or anfwer to; fo much it wants of perfection, and fo much it is different from its *archetype.*

2dly, That thofe, whofe *idea* of gold is only referred to, folely refpects, and is abfolutely terminated upon the *real effence* of gold, which is unknown to them; fc. thofe who when they think of gold, endeavour to think of nothing but the *real effence* of it : thefe men, I fay, are fo far from having an *adequate idea* of gold, that they have no manner of idea of it, nor indeed any idea at all : for fince of that which is unknown in things we can have no idea, we can never think of any thing if we do not know it. And fince their idea of *gold* extends to *nothing* but what is unknown; it is plain there is nothing of that which is in gold in this *idea*; there is correfpondency betwixt the type, and its pretended *archetype*, no likenefs, no refemblance. It is no more the idea of gold than of any other thing; and indeed it is the *idea* of nothing; fc. no *idea*, but a delufion of the mind, thinking it has an idea when it has none.

3dly, Thofe whofe *idea* of *gold* is referred to *fenfible qualities* of it only, or its active and paffive powers difcoverable by us; fc. thofe who when they think of *gold*, think of nothing but thefe: fuch men, I fay, though they have fomething of that which is in gold in their idea, yet are far from having an adequate idea of it, for the reafons abovementioned!.

Ibid.

Ibid. line 4. 1. *Sometimes* they are.—Sometimes when men think of fubftances they endeavour to think of nothing but a fuppofed real effence in them.

Ibid. *Sometimes they* are.—§ 8, *page* 403, Thofe who endeavour to copy fubftances.—Sometimes fome men, when they think of fubftances, think of nothing but that collection of that active and paffive powers they obferve in them, and this is all the idea we have of them.

Ibid. line 12. *It is ufual.*—He fuppofes that men generally give names to things only upon account of their fpecific effence; that their names folely refpect them; fo that they would not, for inftance, call a parcel of matter, gold, did they not think it had a certain real effence, which runs through all the parcels of that fort; for its having fuch an effence is what they mean when they give it that name.

Ibid. line 24. And thus they.—Thus they give the name of gold, under which they rank all parcels of matter of that fort. They give it, I fay, to thofe parcels only upon account of a *fpecific real effence,* which they are fuppofed to have, and to be diftinguifhed by from all other parcels of matter.

Ibid. line 41. For then the properties.—He fuppofes the *complex idea* already made by a collection of thofe qualities we have hitherto difcovered in a *fub-ftance,* and that afterwards we find fome others, which might as well be put into the collection, but that they were found out too late: fc. after the *collection* was made.

Ibid. line 59. *That men* fhould.—That they fhould afcribe the diftribution of things into forts to the fpecific effences (one of which is fuppofed to run through every fort and diftinguifh it from all others) as the only caufe of fuch a diftribution.

§ 9, *page* 404, *line* 2. *Could not rationally.*—For the real effence being but one, a fixed and certain thing:

whatever qualities depend upon that, muſt be fixed, certain, and immutable : ſo that every parcel of matter we call *gold,* muſt have the ſame bulk and figure, which we ſee is not ſo.

§ 12, *page* 405, *line* 15. *That ſimple idea.*—Thus when I have the idea of paper being white, I think of a power it hath to produce that ſenſation in me : and the paper hath really juſt ſuch a power extending only to its effect, and no other : for if it extended to other effects alſo, it might produce a ſenſe of other colours as well as whitenefs ; which I ſee it doth not ; ſo that my idea correſponds, anſwers, is agreeable, adequate, and commenſurate, to the power in the paper of which it is the *idea.*

§ 13, *page* 406, *line* 25. *A man has no idea.*—He means of unknown ſubſtratum, of extenſion and ſolidity in matter.

CHAP. XXXII.
Of True and False Ideas.

§ 6, *page* 409, *line* 1. *THESE* ſuppoſitions.—Chiefly of *abſtract complex ideas* ; and the reaſon is, that men being very much given to make theſe *abſtract ideas* ; it is natural for them to ſuppoſe they are agreeable to things without them, for elſe they muſt think they had not made them right.

§ 9, *page* 410, *line* 8. *And every day's.*—Sc. by the frequent occaſions he has to obſerve what names men give to each colour.

Ibid. line 13. *By the objects.*—In which he hath obſerved how men call them.

Ibid. line 15. *Or applies the name.*—Sc. judges that that *idea* he expreſſes by the name *red,* is the ſame *idea*
which

which others expreſs by that name, when it is not ſo, but is that which they expreſs by the name *green.*

§ 12, *page* 411, *line* 14.   In reference.—In reference to the ideas of other men, expreſſed by the ſame names, and looked upon as a ſtandard.

§ 14, *page* 412, *line* 10.   *And thus* anſwering.—This is coincident with *adequate ideas,* c. 30, § 2, *page* 394, and ſo each ſenſation anſwering the power; and with *real ideas,* c. 31, § 2, *page* 397, and thus our *ſimple ideas* are all *real* and *true,* becauſe they *anſwer, &c.*

Ibid. line 13.   *If the mind.*—So judges of them, it makes a falſe judgement, which is all the falſeneſs there can be in *ideas.* Though indeed this falſe notion of them ſerves the uſes of life as well as the true one.

§ 15, *page* 413, *line* 6.   *If the idea of a violet.*—The ſuppoſition is that the *idea,* produced by a Violet in the mind of A, is the ſame that a Marigold produces in the mind of B, and conſequently different from that which a Violet produces in the mind of B, and ſo in like manner, the *idea* produced by a Marigold in the mind of A, is the ſame that a Violet produces in the mind of B, and conſequently different from that which a Marigold produces in the mind of B.   Now though this would breed no confuſion or inconvenience as to the uſes of life, provided A called that *idea* which a Violet produced in him *blue,* as well as B, though it were different from B's *idea*; and that *idea* which the Marigold produced in him, *yellow,* as well as B, though different from B's *idea.*   Yet, notwithſtanding, if A ſhould think his *idea* of *blue and yellow* were the ſame with B's *ideas* of thoſe colours; this would be a falſe judgement of his *ideas,* which is all the *falſeneſs* that can be in them.

§ 18, *page* 414, *line* 12.   *When they put together.*— This and the following inſtance of falſe ideas are coincident with the fantaſtical ones, c. 30, § 2, *page* 397.

BOOK III.   CHAP. I.

Of Words, or Language in General.

§ 5, page 428, line 12. *A*RE all words taken, &c.—
This inference feems to be
too general; for every man, whether there were
any words or articulate founds ufed or not, would
underftand his own thoughts; the ufing fuch words,
therefore, to exprefs infenfible things, argues only the
defect in language, but not our want of knowledge of
fuch things, unlefs we could fuppofe fuch as are deaf
and dumb have no thoughts or confcioufnefs of the actions of their own minds; or that there is a natural connexion between the founds and the thoughts themfelves,
both which are demonftrably falfe.*

Ibid. line 13. *Spirit in its primary.*—Thefe words indeed feem to prove that *fenfible ideas* were the firft in the
mind; for men would not have taken from them words
to exprefs their *ideas* of *immaterial fubftances*, had they not
been known and familiar to the mind before fuch *ideas*
of *immaterial fubftances*. But as for the metaphorical
words he mentions, *adhere, conceive, inftill*, they feem
not to have been made by the firft beginners of languages, but to have been brought in afterwards by
poets, orators, rhetoricians, to pleafe and gratify the fan-
cies of men, and adorn and embellifh difcourfe.

CHAP. II.

Of the Signification of Words.

§ 2, page 431, line 13. *N*OR can any one apply.—
He may pronounce the
word like a parrot without knowing what *idea* it ftands

* Ch. 2, § 1.

for:

for : but if he do apply it to any *idea* at all, it muſt be to one of his own *ideas.*

Ibid. line 15. *For this would be to make.*—This would be to be capable of doing a thing which would wholly deſtroy the uſe of language, and conſequently be a re-flection on the Author of nature for contriving it in ſuch a manner.

CHAP. III.

Of General Terms.

§ 9, *page* 439. AN *abſtract idea* is nothing elſe but the repreſentation or reſemblance in the mind of a ſingle or particular viſible object, when the object itſelf is not *preſent* does not actually affect the eye.

There can be no *general* or *abſtract ideas* in the author's ſenſe, becauſe no men can think of more than *one* thing at *one* inſtant, and therefore cannot form a *general* or *abſtract idea.**

§ 12, *page* 442, *line* 15. *Whereby it is evident.*— The ſeries and force of this reaſoning is this : *to be of any ſpecies* is the *ſame* as to have a *right* to the *name* of *that ſpecies.* To have *right* to the *name* of a *ſpecies* is to have a *conformity* to the *abſtract idea* of that *ſpecies;* to have a *conformity* to the abſtract *idea* of that *ſpecies* is to take all in that the *abſtract idea* contains ; *ergo,* to have the *eſſence* of a *ſpecies* is the ſame as to have all that the *abſtract idea* of that ſpecies contains and no more ; ſo that the *eſſence* of a *ſpecies,* and the *abſtract idea* of it, are the ſame.

§ 12, *page* 444, *line* 4. For *the having the eſſence.* —Having the *eſſence* of a *ſpecies*—being of that *ſpecies*

* Lee, p. 204.

—having a *right* to the *name* of that *species*—having a *conformity* to the *abstract idea* to which that name is annexed : *ergo,* having the *essence* of a *species*—having a *conformity* to the *abstract idea.*

    Ibid. line 4. *That the essences of the sorts.*—In order to understand this expression, we may observe, 1ft, that as the word *idea* often signifies in this author a *real quality* of a thing without us, as well as our thoughts and notion of that *quality;* so the term *abstract idea* may signify a collection of *real qualities* co-existing in a thing without us and common to it with other things, as well as our complete thought or notion of those *qualities.*

    2dly, That *essence* and *sort* or *species* in this expression may be referred either to our minds, or to things without us ; if they are referred to our minds, the meaning of the expression is, that it is the *essence* or nature of a *sort* to be the *workmanship of our understanding,* to be a *thought* of our *minds,* which we might have, though nothing now existed without us. And in this sense it would more proper to say, that a *sort* is an *abstract idea;* for it is the very same thing with it. If they are referred to things without us (as when it is said, the *essence of a sort of things is an abstract idea)* the meaning of the expression is, that the common essence and nature of all those things (i. e. all that we know, conceive, or think of them) which has occasioned us to sort them together is only a collection of *real, secondary, sensible qualities,* co-existing in them all, and in no other things : in this sense it would be more proper to say, that the *essence* of all things *sorted* is an *abstract* idea, or a collection of *real, &c.* qualities.

    The simple thoughts of these single *qualities* make up our complex thought of the whole collection, to which thought we give a *name,* which mediately or secondarily signifies the collection of *qualities* also ; and hence the collection is called the *nominal essence* of those things (because it is that *essence,* which the *name* stands for in opposition to the *real essence,* or internal constitu-

tion

fion of them, which we have no knowledge or thought
of, and consequently can make no *name* for.

Ibid. page 446, *line* 28. *Now since nothing.*—This
reasoning seems not valid, for it may be said, that to
have a *conformity, &c.* and to have the *essence, &c.* are
still different things, though both are required to the
being of a *man.* It might perhaps be made valid thus
—since *nothing can be a man* but only by having a *conformity, &c.* and nothing can be a man but what has
the *essence, &c.* Sc. since both these things, hitherto
appearing *different* are the only way for any thing to be
a *man,* they must needs be *one* and the *same* thing. It
might have been sufficient to prove this point to have
shewn, that these *abstract ideas* are *all* that we think of
particular things, all the conceptions we have of them
when we make them into *sorts.*

§ 13, *page* 447, *line* 7. The forting of them.—
Though nature has made them thus *alike,* they could
not have been *sorted,* or had *general names* given, but
for the mind of man.

Ibid. page 448, *line* 40. *He will never be able.*—He
means, I presume, because these *supposed real essences*
are unknown, so that we cannot tell in any of them,
for instance, when there is *all* of it, and when not.

§ 14, *page* 448, *line* 12. *It having been more.*—
This instance proves that these contending parties have
different ideas of a *man.* For whereas a certain shape of
the body is a leading quality in this *idea,* one of these
parties it is plain admits of a greater latitude in that
shape than another.

Ibid. It is both obscure and confounding to say that
abstract ideas are the very *essence* of those things which
are sorted; for this does not keep up the *difference* between the act of the mind and its object; for the *idea*
surely is in the *mind,* and the properties which make

the *effence* are in the *objects*, and would be there whether
we conceived them or not.*

§ 15, *page* 449. Effence is the very nature of any
being, whether it be actually exifting or no.†
    Ibid. Here (not to mention that it is not extraor-
dinary for the fignification of a derivative word, efpecially in a philofophical *fenfe*, (acceptation) to differ
widely from the grammatical meaning according to the
form it is derived in) the word Being, I think is equivocal, and fignifies the internal unknown conftitution of
things, lefs properly, at leaft left commonly, than any
other thing. But granting that effence, being, and the
internal unknown conftitution of fubftances are properly
the fame thing : fince this internal unknown conftitution once exifted not, and yet was known then in the
divine intellect, it muft have been in idea there ; fo that
at laft in any acceptation of the word we muft refolve
the effence of things into idea, and make it the fame
with their nature.‡
    Ibid. If effence and exiftence have different mean-
ings (as in propriety it feems they fhould) by effence
I think can only be meant, the abftract natures of
things, or the ideas of the things in the divine intellect,
which were before the things exifted.§
    Mr. Locke rather takes effence for the being of any
thing ; though we ufually fay, fuch a property is of the
nature or efience of a thing, taking either word indifferently ; but never that it is of the being of it, which
rather imports its exiftence.
    It would have feemed ftrange if Dr. Clarke had
called his moft excellent bcok, a demonftration of the
effence or internal unknown conftitution (inftead of the
being and attributes) of God. And then if fubftances

* Lee, p. 205.   † Ibid. p. 23.   ‡ Baxt. N. p. 144.
§ Baxt. p. 143.

                                                        have

have unknown effences and other things have not, it will follow that there are two different fpecies of effences, or that other things befides fubftances have no effence at all. It was this put Mr. Locke upon the diftinction of real and nominal effences; and afferting that all our moral and mathematical ideas, as of virtue, vice, &c. a cube, a fquare, &c. (things of as fixed and immutable natures, as any that can be named) having only according to his diftinction nominal effences, are nothing but the mere arbitrary compofitions of ideas in our minds; which admitted, would be of the greateft differvice both in philofophy and practice.*

Some men pretend to have Mr. Locke's authority for infinuating that the unknown conftitution of things is in itfelf nothing, and that fubftance or what he calls fub-ftratum, is but empty found. But they are miftaken, for Mr. Locke allows that the internal, &c. is *fome-thing*, upon which their difcoverable qualities are owned to depend; and this other thing, if we fpeak of it at all, muft be called fubject, fupport, fubftance, or fome fuch name; and though we have no particular idea of it, yet we know that it is, unlefs properties could fubfift by themfelves, and if there be neither property nor fubject, there would be nothing left to exift.†

§ 17, *page* 450, *line* 19. The frequent production. —See § 14. The force of this argument I take to be this, it is impoffible there fhould be a fet, determinate number of thefe *effences*, becaufe thefe productions are daily inftances of *new effences*, which appears from hence, that they have not the properties of *the old effences*.

§ 19, *page* 452. There is but one being which in-cludes exiftence in the very effence of it, and i. e. God. But the actual exiftence of every creature is very dif-

---

* Baxt. p. 147.   † Ibid. p. 144.

tinct from its effence, for it *may be* or *may not be,* as God pleafe.*

§ 19, *page* 452, *line* 43.   And is founded on the.— This feems not to be true, becaufe the *idea* might fub-fift in men's minds, though they never expreft it by any *fign.*

CHAP. IV.

Of the Names of Simple Ideas.

§ 6, *page* 455. THIS definition is the definition of a word, not a thing, that is a fub-ftance or a mode of it.   Definition is ufually reckoned the name of a propofition, in which the property or properties of a thing is fo fet forth as to diftinguifh it from every thing elfe ; or in fhewing the effence of that thing, or the genus and differentia, which is much the fame.

§ 7, *page* 455.   Single qualities are undefinable, 1ft, Becaufe definition is an explanation ; but fingle quali-ties cannot be explained, becaufe they are fenfible, and muft be known by the help of proper organs, and when they are fo known, no words can make them plainer. 2dly, Becaufe the reafon or caufe of them cannot be known at all.

§ 8, *page* 455, *line* 1. *The not obferving.*—Thefe inftances feem not pertinent ; for the philofophers, ef-pecially the *Cartefians,* in defining the words *motion and light,* did not intend to raife or produce in men's minds the *ideas* thofe terms ftand for, but only to fhew the effects of the one and caufe of the other : fc. what follows in matter from its having the affection called

* Watts Log. p. 11.

motion,

motion, or its being in that ftate in the prefent fyftem of things ; and what fort of particles they are that raife that *idea* in our minds we call *light*.

CHAP. V.

Of the Names of Mixed Modes and Relations.

§ 2, *page* 463, *line* 5. WHEREIN they differ.— The author feems to confound making of *complex ideas* with *abftracting* them ; for the *abftracting* of *complex ideas* is as much the work of the underftanding, as the *abftracting* of *fimple* ones, though *making* is not.

§ 3, *page* 463. *Mixed modes* are no more creatures of the underftanding than fubftances ; for a man can as eafily diftinguifh between *virtue and vice*, as he can between fome animals, plants, &c. by the light of nature, and fuch rules as God has given every man by which to compare actions : and if *abftract ideas* be only the figns of *real actions*, the actions applied to particular cafes, appear as manifeftly different as the fubftances themfelves. And as barbarous as fome men are pleafed to reprefent others, yet moft fort of actions that are efteemed good or bad, are fo diftinguifhed (however different their names for them are) all the world over ; and therefore are not voluntary or arbitrary.*

§ 8, *page* 467, *line* 19. *And the verfura* (a fort of brokening) *of the Romans,* &c.—This does not prove that the *ideas* of the actions were *voluntary* and *arbitrary*, for let the *Romans* or *Jews* have agreed upon any other words to fignify thofe actions, yet the actions would have been the fame : nor can I learn, how the names

* Lee, p. 210.

of

of theſe mixed actions tye the actions together, more than the names of ſubſtance s do their properties.*

§ 9, *page* 468, *line* 20.   Who makes the.—See c. 3, § 14.

§ 12, *page* 470.   I always thought it as impoſſible for a man to form any notion of *juſtice and gratitude* without comparing his own, or the ſenſible *actions* of others with the *laws of nature*, which incline him to the practice of them, as of a horſe and iron, without *ſeeing* them, or having them repreſented to him by ſomewhat like them.   For it ſeems plain to me, that theſe which he calls *mixed modes*, are nothing elſe but *mixed actions*, with their circumſtances, and that we have no *idea* at all of them in our minds upon hearing or reading their *general names*, till they are reſolved into particular *actions*, and their *modes* which conſtitute them.†

§ 15, *page* 472, *line* 9.   Unleſs a man will.—He intimates that if we endeavour to frame the *complex ideas* before we learn the *names*, we ſhall be apt to make ſuch *new* and *ſtrange* compoſitions, as will be utterly unknown to others, and uſeleſs to us in our converſation with them.

CHAP. VI.

Of the Names of Subſtances.

§ 1, *page* 474, *line* 21.   T HAT might be a ſun.—Sc. one man may have one *abſtract idea* of a globe of fire, and another have another, different from the former, which could not be if the *abſtract idea* of a globe of fire (in which all globes of

* Lee, p. 210.   † Ibid. p. 211.

fire

fire are comprehended (were an *idea* of the *real* nature of it, for that being but *one*, there could then be but one *abstract idea.*

§ 2, *page* 474, *line* 7. *This though it be all.*—He now speaks of the lowest *nominal essence* that can be made in the *predicamental* scale, which contains indeed all that we know of *substances* ranked under it. As the *nominal essence* expressed by the word *gold*, contains all that we know of particular pieces of *gold*, ranked under it. But highest in the predicamental scale, the *nominal essence* expressed by the word *tree*, for instance, doth not contain all that we know of an oak, ash, elm, &c. ranked under it.

§ 4, *page* 475. Every thing that is *essential*, is essential to individuals, for *essential* is only the title or name we give to those *properties and qualities*, which distinguish *individuals* from all other *individuals* that want them; and *properties* are not in *generals*, but in *individuals.**

And the measure and boundary of each species will not be the abstract ideas, but the properties of each individual, which would be in them whether we conceived them or not.†

Ibid. line 15. *Other creatures.*—The shape of my body may be lost by an accident, but may also be made to belong to a parcel of matter united to a spirit very *different* from mine, and from any human soul; which is still some further proof, that it is not *essential* to my body; the same may be said of the reason of my mind.

Ibid. line 19. *None of these are essential*, &c.— Though disease or accident may take away man's life, yet it cannot annihilate his soul, the thinking substance, nor destroy those thoughts, by which he is *distinguish-able* from all bodies, and all other *individual spirits*; and

---

thoſe properties ſo retained we call the *eſſence of the in-dividual ſpirit.* None of theſe alterations are made merely by our thoughts; the mind has no more to do therein but to obſerve the properties in each individual, as made by nature, and give the ſubſtances wherein they are common or different names.*

§ 5, *page* 476, *line* 1. *Thus if the idea.*—Sc. If I take a thing in my hand, and ſay this is a *body*, then *extenſion* alone, or *extenſion* and *ſolidity both* (according as my *abſtract idea of body* is) is *eſſential* to it, ſc. while I ſuppoſe it to be a *body* and no longer.

Ibid. line 9. *Should there be found.*—A parcel of matter conſidered as ſuch can never want any thing *eſſential* to it; it is what the *Creator* deſigned it, perfect in its kind. But if any ſort of *matter*, iron, be propoſed as a *ſtandard*, it may be void of ſomething *eſſential* to its being of that *ſort.*

Ibid. page 447, *line* 4. *Or could it be demanded.*—There could be no room for this queſtion till ſome ſort of *matter*, iron, be propoſed as a *ſtandard* and meaſure of *eſſential* and *ſpecific*, from which it might *eſſentially* and *ſpecifi-cally* differ.

Ibid. line 9. *For I would.*—Vide c. 3, § 13. He will never be able to know.

Ibid. line 13. *All ſuch patterns.*—Sc. had we not made an *abſtract complex idea* (conſiſting of a particular ſet of qualities co-exiſting united) as a *pattern* and *ſtandard* to which all parcels of *matter* were to be re-duced that had that particular ſet of qualities. Were it not, I ſay, for this *abſtract idea*, all the qualities of this parcel of matter, I cut my pen with, would be one as *eſſential* to it as another. But this *abſtract idea* being made, whenever I ſuppoſed the parcel of matter, I mentioned, to be agreeable to it, its *quality* of obeying the loadſtone is *eſſential* to it: ſc. it is more *eſſential* to

* Lee, p. 215.

its

ɪts being *iron*, than to its *malleablenefs*, though not to
its being a parcel of *matter*, or metal.

Ibid. line 16. *And every thing.*—Sc. one thing as
much as another, though in reality nothing at all.

This one general fentiment feems to run through this
excellent performance, viz. *that the effences of things are
utterly unknown to us, and therefore all our pretences to
diftinguifh the effences of things can reach no farther than
mere nominal effences, &c.* Now that we may do juſtice
to this great author, we muſt confider that he confines
this fort of difcourfe only to the *effence of fimple ideas*,
the *effence of fubftances*, as appears cap. 4, § 6, lib. 3, for
he allows the *names of mixed modes always to fignify the
real effences of their fpecies*, cap. 5, and that in the diftinction of their effences, *there is generally lefs confufion
and uncertainty than in natural*, cap. 6, § 40, 41.
Though it muſt be confeſſed he fcarce makes any diftinction between the *definition of the name*, and the *definition of the thing*, cap. 4; and fometimes the current
of his difcourfe decries the knowledge of effences in
fuch general terms as may juſtly give occafion to
miſtake.*

We can demonſtrate feveral eternal truths concerning the natures or effences of things. For to
fhew the neceſſity or neceſſary confiſtence of thefe
eternal properties (i. e. as being originally, eternally
confiſtent ideas) is to demonſtrate eternal truths concerning their natures.†

§ 6, *page* 477. A late author hath rightly obferved
that effence is explained by the chief and radical property of a thing, or all the properties of it. Hence
the chief and radical property of a thing is the effence
in idea, though the thing fhould not exiſt nor have any
internal unknown conſtitution. Effence is very diffe-

---

* Vide Watts Log. p. 114.   † Baxt. p. 302.

rent from exiftence, the effence or nature of things is invariable, and their exiftence only contingent.*

Ibid. line 9.   But effence.—Becaufe even thefe real *effences* are not *effential* to, or infeparable from any particular parcel of matter; for it is not *effential* to the parcel of matter I have now on my finger, to have that particular difpofition of its infenfible parts that it has, it might as well have had, or ftill have, another.

Ibid. line 12.   *Properties belong only to fpecies, not to individuals.*—But let a man try to fatisfy another's hunger by his own eating, or to make another confcious of his pleafures or pains, and he will find that properties belong to *individual fubftances* or particular men, and not to the *fpecific name*, or general word *man.*

Ibid. line 12. *Properties belonging.* — By *properties* he means *fenfible difcoverable qualities,* which he hath already fhewn are no otherwife *effential* to individuals than as they are fuppofed to be of a *fpecies.*   And fince thefe *properties* have an infeparable connexion with the effence called the *real* they muft ftand and fall together.   So that if *properties* are *effential* to things only upon the fuppofal of their being of a *fpecies,* the *real effence* can be *effential* upon no other account.

Ibid. page 472, *line* 8. *But there is.*—He fhould have faid here *to which any of thefe real effences* (from thefe qualities flow) *are fo annexed;* for it is of the *real effences* he is now fpeaking.

§ 7, *page* 478, *line* 3. *Subftances are.*—Sc. becaufe it has that *nominal effence;* becaufe that *abftract complex idea* we denote by the word, *horfe, tree, &c.* agrees to it. For this reafon only, upon this ground alone, it is ranked under this *fort,* and not becaufe it has fuch or fuch *real effence,* for that we know nothing of.

* Baxt. p. 152, 301.

§ 9, *page* 480, *line* 44. To try his ſkill.—A man may pretend to diſtinguiſh *ſheep or goats* by their *real eſſences* into ſeveral *ſorts*, when indeed he doth it by their *nominal eſſences*, which are known to him. But theſe animals *Caſſiowary* and *Querechinchio* (which he is ſuppoſed to ſee, and not to know how many or what *ſenſible qualities* make up the *complex idea* that denominates, and bounds the *ſpecies)* he cannot diſtinguiſh, ſo that if another *Caſſiowary* be brought ſomething diſſe-rent from the former, but within the bounds of the *ſpecies*, he will not be able to ſay, whether it be of that ſort, or of the ſort of *Querechinchino's*; hence it appears his pretences are vain, and that he diſtinguiſhes things into *ſorts* by their *nominal eſſences*, and not by their *real*, for if he did it by the *real*, he might as well diſtinguiſh *Caſſiowary* from *Querechinchino* as *ſheep* from *goats*, ſince he knows the *real eſſence* of the two former, as much as that of the two latter.

§ 11, *page* 481, *line* 5. *Evident from.*—The force of the argument lies in this. We cannot rank ſpirits well, and diſtinctly into different ſorts, becauſe we have ſo few ideas of reflexion that are different to make various combinations of. This ſhews that when we do rank and ſort things, we do it by ſuch combinations of *ideas*, and by the *real eſſences* of things : for they are doubtleſs as diſtinct and different, and as much unknown to us, in *ſpirits*, as in *corporeal* ſubſtances, though the *qualities* we attribute to them are not.

Ibid. page 482, *line* 54. *Who yet.*—He ſeems to ſuppoſe that all the difference between *God* and the *higheſt* order of *ſpirits*, in our *idea* of each of them, is only one degree of *exiſtence*, *knowledge*, &c. But is vaſtly more than ſo, being a difference between *finite* degrees, and *infinite*, which bear no proportion, if thoſe words, *infinitely more remote*, reſpect the number of *ſimple ideas*, which ſhould be put into the *idea* of *God*, more than into the *idea* of other *ſpirits :* it muſt be confeſſed that upon this ac-

count

count our *ideas of God* and of other *spirits* are very in-
diftinct, for want of that vaft number of *ideas* which
fhould enter into the *idea of God,* and which we have
not put to it.

§ 13, *page* 483. *Ice* is without doubt a different
fort or *fpecies* from water, becaufe it has diftinct properties; but the man that calls it *hardened water* is no
more miftaken than if he had called *melted wax, fluid
wax;* from whence I infer that giving *names* depends
upon every one's experience; but not making *effences;*
that is a work of *nature,* not of mere *thoughts or ideas.**

§ 26, *page* 490. *line* 39. *Whereby it is evident.*—
It is not evident that thofe who rejected the foetus made
only the *outward figure,* and not the *faculty of reafoning
effential* to a *man;* they might notwithftanding make
reafon as *effential* as the others, who received the *foetus.*
But a certain fhape of the body (admitting indeed of
fome variety, but within fome certain bounds) being a
leading *quality* in the *idea* of *man;* and the only indica-
tion we have that *reafon* will be joined to fuch a body;
thofe who reject the *foetus* admit not fo great a latitude
in that *fhape* as thofe who receive it.

§ 28, *page* 492, *line* 4. *To the making.*—Thefe
words till you come to in *the firft of thefe,* feem put as
it were in a parenthefis; and by the words any *nominal
effence,* is meant any one, and the fame *nominal effence.*

Ibid. line 5. *Firft that the ideas.*—This is more than
to fay, that a *nominal effence* is a *complex idea.*

Ibid. line 8. *Exactly the fame.*—Sc. as to fort and
kind.

Ibid. line 9. *For if two abftract.*—Thefe words relate
to the foregoing; *fecondly, that the particular ideas fo
united,* and only to them.

* Lee, p. 217.

Ibid.

Ibid. line 11. *In the first of these.*—These words refer to those in the beginning of the §, *these nominal essences of substances.*

§ 38, *page* 501, *line* 16. *In the different.*—So, because the collections of *simple ideas* expressed by the word *flock* are almost the same, denoted by the word *hound*; these are not distinct *species* of animals; whereas the collections of *simple ideas* denoted by the words, *spaniel and elephant,* are different, therefore they are different *sorts* of animals.

§ 43, *page* 503, *line* 22. *But because.*—Because it is difficult by known names to lead men into the thoughts of things stript of those *specifical* differences we give them; and yet it is necessary that men should be lead into those thoughts in treating of *specific ideas and names:* upon these accounts, it is better to use examples than words in this matter.

Ibid. line 24. *To make the different.*—That is to shew how the consideration the mind has of *specific ideas* we call *modes,* and their *names* at one time is different from what it has of them at another : as also the consideration the mind has of these *ideas* is different from that which it has of the *ideas of substances.*

VOL. II. CHAP. VIII.

Of Abstract and Concrete Terms.

§ 1, *page* 4. BY *concrete terms* is commonly meant the names of substances, given them either on the account of one quality or property, or their relation to one another ; and by *abstract terms* the common names of those qualities, properties, or actions observed in substances compared with one another, in

those

thofe qualities, properties, or actions, without regard to any other of properties or actions.*

§ 2, *page* 5, *line* 13. *We have very few,* &c.—The reafon is becaufe no two or more fubftances can fo eafily be like one another in every one of their properties or qualities, as they may in fome one *leading* quality ; and therefore it is obfervable, that where an offer has been made at abftract terms from fubftances, it is only to exprefs fome *peculiar* quality, and not all the *qualities* ; as in *aquofity, fierinefs,* &c.

CHAP. IX.

Of the Imperfection of Words.

§ 2, *page* 6, *line* 1. *AS to the firft of thefe,* &c.— This is not clear ; 1, Becaufe deaf and dumb perfons, without doubt, remember their own thoughts without words. 2dly, When perfons talk to themfelves their thoughts precede their words, or excite their remembrance of their words, juft contrary to what occurs in converfation or reading.†

§ 5, *page* 7. The doubtfulnefs of words feems rather to *arife from* the different experience of the perfons ufing, hearing, or reading thefe words, than the uncertainty of their fignification.

The cafes in which they are generally doubtful are, 1. When words are ufed, which in the common language of the country have very different fignifications. 2. When words are relative, and the reference is different in the mind of the fpeaker from the hearer. 3. When words may be taken with a lefs or greater latitude, as religion, grace, faith, &c. 4. When words are ufed to fignify actions, that agree in fome particular circumftances or modes with other

* Lee, p. 221.   † Ibid.

actions,

⅃ions, that do not agree with them in all, and are
therefore in ſtriɕtneſs, to be reputed metaphorical.*

Ibid. page 8, *line* 13. *Where the ſignification.*—The
author never mentions this caſe in the following diſ-
courſe : but he means, I ſuppoſe, that this happens in
ſubſtances where the *names* ſignify a collection of qualities which are different from the *real eſſence* of a thing,
being the effects of it.

§ 6, *page* 8.   I. *Becauſe of that great compoſition.*—
The multiplicity of the ideas cannot be the cauſe of
the doubtfulneſs of ſuch words ; but either the neglect,
ignorance or prejudice of the perſon ſpeaking or
hearing.†

§ 7, *page* 9.   II. *Becauſe the names, &c.*—This
too ſeems rather imputable to the prejudices of the
ſeveral perſons ſpeaking or hearing, and not to the
words themſelves, or the want of *ſtandards :* for I reckon
the *ſtanderds* of moral actions to be as fixed, as of ſubſtances natural or artificial ; or even of *ſimple ideas,* or
qualities.‡
   All men, free from prejudice, can as eaſily diſtinguiſh
between moral good and evil, as between white and
black, from their relation to the laws of nature, and the
land, which is as unalterable by the power of names, or
the ideas of particular perſons, as the properties or
eſſences of ſubſtances. §
   Ibid. line 21. *What the word murther, &c.*—This
is true, but not to the main purpoſe : for the whole
queſtion is, Whether thoſe actions of which theſe words
are the ſigns, be not immutably agreeable or diſagree-
able to the laws of God, and conſequently good or evil;
and whether thoſe laws of nature be not as certain and
fixed, as the very laws of motion ?||

---

* Lee, p. 222.   † Ibid. p. 223.   ‡ Ibid.
§ Lee, p. 223. || Ibid. p. 225.

§ 8, *page* 10.   It is not at all material whether the
word be proper or not in its original signification.
Though the word *justice* be derived from *jus*, which
signifies *broth* as well as right, yet being commonly
used for the virtue of giving every one his due, that
makes it proper.*

§ 9, *page* 10, *line* 35.   *And hence we see, &c.*—He
should have distinguished between the common or necessary principles, and controversial points : for however large the commentators have been in the latter,
yet in the former, which are the main, we may observe
almost an universal consent, allowing something for the
manner of expression.†

§ 11, *page* 12, *line* 5.   *The names of substances.*—
But neither are the names of substances doubtful; because they are supposed conformable to their real ef-
sences as made by nature; for the names of substances are given them by particular persons, according
to the properties they observe in them, common to
other individual substances.‡

§ 23, *page* 21.   *Since then the precepts, &c.*
—Yet ought we as much to adore the goodness of
God for his special providence about those ancient
writings, for the preserving a lasting standard for our
faith and manners.§

CHAP. X.

Of the Abuse of Words.

§ 5, *page* 24.   THE author seems guilty of this himself in his use of the word *idea*, for
he uses it sometimes for the act of perception, thus

---

* Lee, p. 225.   † Ibid. p. 226.   ‡ Ibid.   § Ibid. p. 228.

2   *sensation*

fenfation is an *idea*; fometimes for the immediate objects of that perception, thus *thoughts* are *ideas*; at other times for the qualities or actions in objects, whether known or perceived by us or not; thus *figure*, *motion*, *bulk*, &c. are *ideas*, though not known.*

§ 6, *page* 25, *line* 22. *Logick* is the art of ufing reafon well in our inquiries after truth, and the communication of it to others.†

§ 15, *page* 30. We have no idea either of *matter* or *body* in general, becaufe they are only the names of fubftances; but only of the particulars that have thofe common names, and fo every fingle parcel of *matter* has as good right to the name of *body*, as every fingle *body* has to the common name of *matter*.

§ 17, *page* 32, *line* 27. *Why might not Plato.*— The force of this reafoning feems to be this: if the word *man* was thought to denote nothing but a *complex idea* of qualities difcoverable in a certain fpecies of things, it might as well ftand for *Plato's* as for *Ariftotle's*; for each of thefe is a *complex idea* of that *fpecies* we are of. The reafon therefore why it does not feem to ftand fo well for the one as the other is, becaufe it is fuppofed to denote the *real effence* of this *fpecies*; and one of thefe *ideas* is thought to come nearer this *real effence* than another. But it may here be faid, that though the word *man* be fuppofed to denote only the moft exact, perfect, diftinguifhing, *complex idea* of qualities obfervable in a fort of things; *Ariftotle's idea* even in this refpect might be preferred before *Plato's*.

* Lee, p. 230. Vide c. 11, § 27. ‡ Watts Log. p. 1.

CHAP. XI.

Of the Remedies of the foregoing Imperfections and Abuses.

§ 20, *page* 52, *line* 17. **F**OR *it is the shape.*—The oppofition is not well made betwixt the *fhape* and the *reafoning faculty*, in reference to the *determining* of the *fpecies*; for *reafoning* may go as far toward that, as the *fhape* even in the *idea* of thofe who kill thefe monftrous births; *fhape* therefore in their opinion rather *indicates* than *determines* the *fpecies*; fc. is the only fign we have to know when *reafon* will be joined to the *animal* body.

The common definition of man is very faulty, animal rationale; becaufe the animal is not rational; the rationality of man arifes from the mind to which the animal is united. 2. Becaufe if a fpirit fhould be united to a horfe, and make it a rational being, furely this would not be a man. It is evident therefore that the peculiar fhape muft either enter into the definition of a man to render it juft and perfect; and for want of a full defcription thereof all our definitions are defective.*

BOOK IV. CHAP. I.

Of Knowledge in General.

§ 2, *page* 59. **K**NOWLEDGE confifts in our perception of the *relation* that fubftances have to their own modes to us, or one another: and all *truth* is only joining or difjoining thefe fubftances according to fuch relation.†

§ 7, *page* 64, *line* 2. *That of actual.*—Here we may obferve that the author does not fay, as in three

---

* Watts Log. Not. p. 109.   † Lee, p. 235.

preceding

preceding cafes, that there is an *agreement* or *difagree-ment* betwixt our *ideas*; for there are no two ideas or thoughts of the mind compared together, as in the former cafes, but one idea (or thought) compared as it were with fome *real* thing exifting without us, which produced it in our minds, and anfwers to it, as a caufe to its effect. As therefore in three former cafes we may have intuitive knowledge of general propofitions by a perception of the agreement or difagreement of our *ideas* (or thoughts of our minds) which are all ab-ftract, and do not fuppofe the exiftence of any things at all without us, now we have thefe thoughts, though they were perhaps the firft occafion of our getting many of them; which knowledge is the confequence of the *ideas* which are in our minds producing there by their agreement or difagreement, perceived *general* and certain propofitions. So in this fourth cafe, we can only have fenfitive knowledge of *particular* propofitions (fc. that fuch and fuch a particular thing exifts without us) and that not only by perceiving any agree-ment or difagreement of *ideas* (or thoughts in our minds) of which there is in this cafe no comparifon made, but by perceiving, fometimes ideas or thoughts are raifed in our minds, and affect us with pleafure or pain, whether we will or no: which muft be owing to things exifting without us, and operating upon us; which *knowledge* is the confequence of the exiftence of things producing *ideas* in our minds, by our fenfes; and though it is not altogether fo certain as intuitive *knowledge*, yet it is an affurance that deferves the name of *knowledge*.*

Ibid. Real exiftence can never be proved merely by ideas, becaufe we can never have any ideas at all of fubftances, and confequently not of their relation to their own properties or modes, or to other fubftances:

---

* Vide B. 4, c, 11, § 12, &c.

this,

this, I fay, cannot be proved, becaufe there will always be wanting an idea by which we muft prove, or explain that relation.*

§ 8, *page* 66.	2. All the *habitual knowledge* we can have of any of the properties of fubftances except they be vifible, muft be gained by rational inferences, that fuch and fuch caufes will produce fuch and fuch effects, or fuch effects argue fuch caufes, which are maxims, when applied to particulars.†

CHAP. II.
Of the Degrees of our Knowledge.

§ 1, *page* 69. *INTUITIVE knowledge* is not *real* but upon fuppofition of the truth of the fenfes; nor any propofition true or falfe but upon fuppofition of things without us, and that our *fenfes are true*; which I am confident cannot be proved by way of *ideas*; for the *ideas* are only the figns of the things, as words are the figns of *ideas*; but neither *ideas* or *words* are figns of any thing, if the *things* themfelves be not fuppofed, and confequently no *propofition* can truly be formed about them.‡

§ 2, *page* 70. If *demonftrative knowledge* be of any ufe, we muft prefuppofe the truth of the fenfes as well in this as in *intuitive knowledge*.§

For in each ftep of the *demonftration* there muft be an *intuitive knowledge*, or rather a *fenfitive knowledge*, a perception by the fenfes: otherwife the mind could not with any certainty judge of the connexion between the feveral objects in the progreffion of its thoughts.‖

* Lee, p. 238.	† Ibid. p. 289.	‡ Ibid. p. 240.
§ Lee, p. 241.	‖ Ibid. p. 242.

§ 11,

§ 11, *page* 74, *line* 2. *And not quantity.*—Thefe words refer only to the word *counted*, and not to *made*, and the meaning is this : we do not reckon two white-nesses to be different becaufe we know the precife number of corpufcles which produce each of them, but becaufe our fenfes perceive each of them to be *diftinct ideas*, which fince our fenfes cannot do in the moft minute degrees and differences in *whitencfs*, therefore this is not a thing capable of demonftration.

§ 14, *page* 76. *Senfitive knowledge* is really the foundation both of *intuitive* and *demonftrative.**

Ibid. page 77, *line* 8. *This certainty is as great.*—This is a very obfcure expreffion ; the meaning of which feems to be this ; when I remove my body near to fomething, which I fancy fends *light* to me at fome diftance, though I am not certain perhaps that there is any thing *really exifting* which enlightened me at a diftance, and to which I approached ; yet I am *certain*, that in all fuch cafes, I fhall feel *pleafure* or *pain*. There is fo much *certainty* as will affure me of *happinefs* or *mifery*. The *certainty* I have therefore in all fuch circumftances may be faid to be commenfurate, or proportionate to, or as great as my *happinefs* or *mifery*; and this is as much *certainty* as we need look after.

C H A P. III.

Of the Extent of Humane Knowledge.

§ 6, *page* 79. IT is an utter impoffibility that matter can ever become by any power a living, felf-moving fubftance ; feeing, matter muft refift all change of its prefent ftate, as it is a folid fubftance.†

Page 80, *note, line* 10. The *whether* fhould not be whether God *can*, but whether he *has* made matter capable

---

* Lee, p. 244.   † Vide Baxt. p. 10, 27, 29.

of

of thinking ; ſc. whether the actions of
which we are conſcious, and for which we have the common
name of thinking, can be performed by mere matter, and
then it will be eaſy to diſcover by all the phænomena in
nature, that matter can no more think than a triangle
can have four angles.　For let matter have what figure,
bulk, motion, or poſition, by parts that can be imagined,
it can no more perceive or be conſcious of its own actions or motions then a ſtone can riſe from the ground
of its own accord, or without the impulſe of another
body.　Whether Omnipotency can add to matter a faculty of thinking, we do not care for diſputing, becauſe
we have no notion of it abſtracted from infinite wiſdom;
and therefore are content to ſay, that according to the
preſent ſtate of the world, and of the experience of our
faculties, that if matter ſhould think, it would as much
ceaſe to be matter, as a triangle would ceaſe to be a triangle that had four angles.*

Ibid.　It is no leſs than a contradiction, &c.
—But there is nothing diſcoverable from the *idea of
God* or *matter* that can make it a contradiction for
God to be *material*, but what will as fully demonſtrate that it is a contradiction for the
ſouls of men to be only *modified matter* ; not from the
idea of God, becauſe the complex idea of God is made
up only of ſimple ideas which we find in ourſelves
magnified in *infinitum* ; not from the *idea* of *matter*, for
we have none that is general, or which extends to all
the individual ſyſtems of it in the univerſe. Ergo, &c.†

The whole argument that matter cannot think nor
move itſelf, concludes in much fewer words from conſidering the endleſs diviſibility of it.‡

Diviſibility is ſuch an affection of ſubſtance as ſhews
on the one hand that matter becauſe diviſible cannot

* Vide Bayle Dict. p. 1924, under Leucippus　Not. on King.
p. 38.　Rel. of Nat. p. 186.　Dr. Clark to Dodwell.　Ditton's
Append. to Reſurr.　Law on King. p. 134.
† Lee, p. 249.　‡ Baxt. N. p. 85.

'think

think or be a living fubftance; and on the other, that
fpiritual fubftance, becaufe thinking cannot be divifible
or have parts.*

Page 83. A man may warrantably fay, that to effect
a contradiction is not the object of any power; nothing
lefs limits Omnipotence: and fuch it is to effect that a
fubftance, which as folidly extended muft refift all
change of ftate, fhould; while remaining folidity extended become of *dull dead earth*, life, fenfe, and fpontaneous motion. (Vide infr. p. 145) So that notwithftanding of this complaint, as if the Bifhop had been
unreafonable in oppofing his conclufion, it appears the
reafon was good, and that he could not go one ftep farther without deftroying the effence of matter, viz. folid
extenfion; and that he had already gone a ftep or two
too far, in making the *fpontaneous mover* in an elephant,
and the external mover in the mechanifm, both of
plants and animals, properties of dull and dead earth.†

But it is perfectly abfurd to fay that infinite power
may fuperadd a property to a fubftance incapable of
receiving it. The fubftance of being firft divifible, and
then the parts of it remaining dead, the property can
have no fubject of inhefion but the junction of dead
parts to dead parts. But that the junction of dead particles, or cohefion of them, itfelf a property, fhould be
the fubject of another property, is an abfurdity Mr.
Locke himfelf hath fufficiently expofed.‡

If this *fubftance* or fubftratum be fo *unknown* a thing,
as Mr. Locke fuppofes, how can I deny any thing concerning it? Or at leaft how can I be fure that God and
the material world have not one common fubftance?
Mr. Locke indeed endeavours to guard his principles
or doctrines from this objection: but I think he neither
does, nor perhaps could he effectually fecure them
fuch unhappy confequences.§

---

* Baxt. p. 106. † Ibid. p. 86.
‡ Baxt. p. 165. § Watts, p. 63.

Solid *extenfion*, and a cogitative power, are real fubftances, for if we nullify them they leave mere nothing
behind them.*

Page 86, *laſt line. But here,* &c.—Here Mr.
Locke fuppoſes that fenfation implies thinking as much
as it implies perception, which, I conceive, is quite
wrong, (vide Baxt. p. 90.) Muſt it not appear more
wonderful to work a piece of mechaniſm in the bounds
of a flea or mite, than in the bounds of an horſe or elephant? Theſe animalcula are therefore as great inſtances
of the wifdom and power of God, as the largeſt living
creatures. Again, does not this mechaniſm as much
require an external immaterial mover, as any mechaniſm whatever, and who fupplies this? laſtly, they
move fpontaneouſly. The objection fuppoſes this :
fpontaneous motion is different from mechanical motion by the terms ; therefore it muſt require a different
immaterial principle. And where is the difficulty in
all this? Or rather in what particular is it not demonſtrative. †

To fuppoſe immortality founded on immateriality is
extremely wrong. The human ſoul being rational, and
the brute ſoul not, the one a moral agent, and the
other not, is the foundation of a very confiſtent and
folid diſtinction between the one and the other as to
immortality.‡

Page 88, *line* 17. *But if you mean,* &c.—Mr.
Locke hath well obſerved, that they are different confiderations that prove the ſoul immortal and immaterial ;
but when he ſays, *that it is* as evident to him, that
brutes reafon in fome inſtances as that they have fenſe
(l. 2. c. 11, § 11.) and here takes it for granted that it
is but *mere matter with fuperadded properties* that thus

---

* Watts, p. 56.
† Vide Baxt. p. 3, 6, N. Keil's Introduct. ad Phyf. lect. 5:
Vide p. 120, v. 1. Bp. Br. on the Und. p. 173. Baxt. p. 108.
Burnet Demonſt. p. 92.
‡ Baxt. p. 108, N.

reafons, tho' he offers no proof of either of thefe af-
fertions; and fince all men fuppofe the matter of the
brute body finally diffipated at death, this gives an ignorant fceptic courage to affirm that it may be fo with
the human foul. It is by no means commendable in
Mr. Locke (who allows the foul to be immaterial,
yet contends it might have been material) to maintain
a point that hath fo bad a tendency, gratis, and barely
for maintaining's fake.*

They who run the parallel between the human
foul and that of brutes, fuppofe ftill the fame powers in both; but furely rationality muft be founded in
fome power which the brute foul as fuch has not : but
granting the activity of the brute foul, when feparated,
this would not certainly infer the human foul is unactive
and impercipient after death, but rather conclude the
contrary the more ftrongly, and perhaps do no differvice to philofophy!†

§ *page 97 line 7. The word fpirit.*—But with fubmiffion, I think no man ever before defended the propriety of an expreffion, exclufive of the truth of it, in a
philofophical controverfy. If the acceptation of a word
is fuch as determines the queftion ; without farther argument, as in this cafe, to juftify the propriety of it
then, is to make the common ufe of language decide
in points of philofophy. If Cicero or Virgil had wrong
ideas as to the immateriality of the foul, tho' they expreffed thefe wrong ideas right, that does not mend the
matter. The difpute between the bifhop and Mr
Locke was, whether matter could think, and not the
claffical acceptation of the word *fpiritus.*‡

Page 103, line 1. It being impoffible for us, &c.—This is
founded upon what Mr. Locke elfewhere endeavours to

* Baxt. p. 87.   † Vid. Baxt. p. 156.   ‡ Baxt. p. 98.

maintain, viz. that our ideas are only *arbitrary* combinations, without connexion to any thing in nature.*

§ 7, *page* 106. All knowledge, or the certainty of
the truth of any propofition, is founded upon a tacit
conftant fuppofition both of the truth of our fenfes and
faculties and of the *real exiftence and real relation* between
thofe things which are affirmed and denied of each
other, and not of their agreement or difagreement in
idea only.†

§ 16. *page* 110. Tho' our knowledge of fubftances
is not adequate, yet if our fenfes and faculties be right,
(which muft be fuppofed in intuitive and demonftrative
knowledge) then fo far as any man's experience reaches,
'tis as certain and real knowledge as what the author
calls *intuitive* and *demonftrative*.‡

§ 18, *page* 111. I take this to comprehend all the
four forts which the author mentions ; but by relative
knowledge he means only the relation of numbers,
lines, figures, angles to each other, which is known
by demonftration, and perhaps alfo of *abftract ideas* in
morality, which can be of no ufe if in *idea* only, without being applied to things without us.§

§ 18, *page* 112, *line* 31. *Where,* &c.—*Ibid. line* 40.
No government, &c.—The two propofitions here mentioned are certainly true, but of no manner of ufe, becaufe the fenfe of them is *identical,* amounting to no
more than this, *where there is no right, there is no
unrighteoufnefs ; and every government governs*.‖

§ 21, *page* 116. If a man doubts of the exiftence of
the things he fees and feels, there is no third idea, but
will need a fourth, nor fourth, but will ftand as much

---

* Baxt. p. p. 86, p. 107. † Lee, p. 250. ‡ Lee, p. 251.
§ Lee, p. 252.   Lee, p. 253.

in need of a fifth, to prove its own exiftence, and fo *in infinitum*; endlefs fcepticifm.*

§ 23, *page* 117, *line* 6. Want of *ideas* is want of knowledge or want of nothing ; and want of knowledge is but another phrafe for ignorance, and differs no other-wife than the want of light does from darknefs; the caufes of ignorance therefore more properly affign'd to the *diftance* or *minutenefs* of fome bodies.†

§ 28, *page* 122. This is not the caufe of our igno-rance, but the very ignorance itfelf, is the imperfection of our faculties that we complain of.†

§ 30, *page* 124. Some men are apt to affign another reafon for this, viz. becaufe many interefts, lufts, and paffions are more apt to mix in other difcourfes than merely in mathematics ; and till all men's interefts be-come the fame, which is impracticable in this world, there would be differences in men's judgements, tho' they were never fo well agreed in the fignification of words.§

CHAP. IV.

On the Reality of Knowledge.

§ 3, *page* 127. BUT this very *conformity* is not dif-coverable in any cafe whatever merely by *ideas*.—There is nothing diftinct from the power of the object, and the perceptions in the mind, and confequently their *conformity* to the reality of the things, or the real power in the objects, cannot be dif-covered for want of fome *real third* thing to make that difcovery.

---

* Lee, p 253. † Ibid. p. 254. § Lce. p. 255.

§ 7, *page* 129. Mixt modes and relations are arbitrary combinations of ideas made without regard to any particular subject in which they may in here; they are evidently their own archetypes, and therefore cannot but be real and positive. They are what they are immutably and universally ; their natures and essences must be the same wherever they are found, so long as the same number of ideas are included under the same word.*

Ibid. The general names of virtues and vices are the signs of the mind, observing such relation to the declared will of God, or our governors, and not the signs of any such fictions as general or *abstract ideas,* for there are none such in the world.†

§ 8, *page* 129. But this knowledge is neither true, real, certain, nor useful ; not true, because truth is the connexion of things by words or other signs really connected or disjoined ; not *certain,* because if things be barely possible, as is supposed in this case, the knowledge can rise no higher in degree than the possibility of the connexion or disjunction, and that's far enough from certainty ; not *real,* because if the archetypes be more accurate than any thing without the mind, they are so far at least not real ; nor *useful,* because if the ideas of actions are beyond any that are or ever were, and the ideas of lines, &c. more exact than any copies of them in bodies are, or ever were, they are not applicable to bodies, and consequently do not answer the end of knowledge, which is usefulness.‡

Ibid. Nor are Tully's Offices less true.—But *Tully's offices* are no farther *true* than 'tis possible for any one to observe them; and no one can rationally judge any thing is possible, that is not, nor ever was done, but by *special revelation.*§

* Note on K. p. 7   † Lee, p. 258.   ‡ Ibid. 159.
§ Ibid.

Since

Since moſt, &c.—But all the general propoſitions that I know are certain and real, are founded on a ſuppoſed real, not an imaginary exiſtence.*

§ 9, *page* 131, *line* 13. *Juſt the ſame is it in moral knowledge.*—The caſe is not altogether the ſame, becauſe the eſſence of a triangle, &c. is its real properties, and thoſe will be unalterable indeed; but if the nominal and real eſſence of virtues and vices be the ſame (as according to the author's principles they are) then if a man alters the name he alters the eſſence in his own judgement; but 'tis otherwiſe in figures, &c.†

§ *page* 132, *line* 5. *Such are our ideas.*—But notwithſtanding this pretended defect, all the real or certain knowledge we have or can have in this world is only of ſubſtances, and their modes on which their relation to us or one another is founded.‡

§ 12, *page* 132. But after all, what he calls ſubſtances are not ſubſtances. Men, gold, iron, &c. are not ſubſtances, but only the common names, the individuals only are real ſubſtances.§

§ 12, *page* 132. A changeling is a particular ſpecies of man, juſt as a perſon of a ſurprizing genius or extraordinary wiſdom is a particular ſpecies of man in the other extreme. Man, is a common name, and every one will give names not according to what things really are in all particulars, but only what they ſeem to be: and therefore a changeling has the eſſence of a man, if by the word eſſence be meant the like properties or qualities by which it may be diſtinguiſhed from every thing elſe that has not the ſame common name; but if by the word eſſence be meant the ſame individual properties and quality, in that ſenſe it is not the ſame eſſence any

* Lee, p. 159 † Ibid. p. 260. ‡ Ibid. 260. § Ibid. p. 261.

more than two men, or two guineas have the same essence.*

What properties are visible those we know, and give them the common name of man, because we know no better, as we call guineas gold, because they are yellow and weighty, tho' they may want, for what we know, the property of being soluble *in aqua regia* †

§ 16, *page* 136. As for monstrous births we judge them a sort of creatures between man and beast, because they partake of the shape and features of both, and therefore esteem them the product of unnatural mixtures.‡

CHAP V.

Of Truth in General.

§ 2, *page* 136. THE common definition of truth is the conjunction or disjunction of things according to the real relation those things have to each other. A mental truth or true mental proposition is, when our thoughts agree with the real relation which the things have to each other of which we think; and a verbal truth is, when the things themselves have that relation really with the words of which they are made the signs agree or disagree; whereas in our notion of truth, 'tis the agreement or disagreement only in ideas or words.§

§ 4, *page* 139. The best way to come at mental propositions is to consider what actions there could be in our minds, if we were born and continued deaf and dumb all our days, which is the case of some: that such affirm and deny or discern the agreement and disagreement of things so far as their observation reaches,

*. Lee, p. 262.   † Ibid.   ‡ Ibid.   § Ibid. p. 264.

there

there is no doubt ; and thofe are properly mental propofitions, and are true when their thoughts agree or
difagree with the real relation there is between the
things they think of.*

CHAP. VI.

Of Univerfal Propofitions, their Truth and Certainty.

§ 5, *page* 146. GENERAL propofitions may be
as certainly known to be true
about fubftances as mathematical propofitions. I am
as ignorant of all the properties belonging to triangles,
&c. as I am of all the active or paffive powers of lead
and gold : but what I know of lead or gold, or other
fubftances, or fo far as my experience goes, I know
as certainly as I do any thing of thofe or any fort of
figures, and can form as many true, certain, and univerfal propofitions concerning them.

CHAP. VII.

Of Maxims.

§ 8, *page* 161. THEY are faid to be *præcognitis*
& præconceffis, becaufe the ac-
tions of children and ideots feem to be governed by
them, even before they can pronounce the words in
which they are expreffed.

§ 9, *page* 162. Children know pleafure and pain,
&c. before they know their names, or form propofitions about them ; yet I guefs they don't in their minds
play with abftract ideas like babies, before they know
that pleafure is pleafure, or pain is pain, &c. and yet

* Lee, p. 265.

that knowledge is but that every thing is the fame with itfelf and not another; and when they grow old enough to be philofophers, they don't need to be taught thofe truths any more than that a ftranger is not their mother, &c. and that is all we mean by faying, thefe truths are *innate.**

§ 11, *page* 165. The main ufe of thefe maxims is, for the folving lefs obvious or more general propofitions into fuch obvious and univerfally acknowledged principles.†

Ibid. page 169, *line* 34. *They fometimes ferve in argumentation to flop a wrangler's mouth.*—But if they flop wranglers mouths 'tis fomething; for that they would not do, if they were not the avowed principles of all the world ; and as for bringing a man into any new knowledge, no body pretends any more than confirming him in the old, which otherwife they might want : and as for *influencing identical predications,* this I take to be a juft and great encomium of them; for all the certainly true propofitions in the world are not clearly perceived to be fuch till they are refolved into fuch identity or the negation of it.‡

§ 13, *page* 172. But all this while there is no fault in the maxims, but in the manner of probation; for in both cafes the queftion is fuppofed, that which fhould be proved is firft granted, and at that rate there is no need of maxims or ideas either.§

§ 18, *page* 175. But all this would have been faved by giving only fome different appellation or the common name; *ex. gr.* as if the child had faid, that a negro is not a white man ; or that changelings are not rational : or that the third was a new fort of rational

* Lee, p. 274. † Ibid. p. 275. ‡ Ibid. p. 274. § Ibid. p. 275.
creature.

creature. The maxims had none of thefe wild infe-rences, but they are all the natural fpawn of *abftraft complex ideas :* and, therefore, notwithftanding thefe objections againft maxims, they are of fingular ufe in the ready proof of fuch propofitions as are not difco-verable by our fenfes where fenfible ideas are not to be had, and that's the utmoft we pretend. *Ex. gr.* We have no idea of the air, of animal fpirits, or of God, yet are certain of their exiftence, by refolving our argu-ments into that maxim, *every effeft muft have a caufe.* But of caufe and effect we have no abftraft general ideas, they are only general relative words or names.*

C H A P. VIII.

Of Trifling Propofitions.

§ 2, *page* 177. IT muft be confeffed that all *identi-cal propofitions* do not fhew him that ufes them, or make another wifer than he was fuppofed to be before : they only direct the attention of what he himfelf or the other faid or thought before, in order to the making himfelf or the other wifer.——Words barely repeated are no propofition at all, 'tis the act of the mind apprehending that relation of the thing to itfelf that makes the propofition, and this is all that is pretended.†

§ 4, *page* 180. Such propofitions are verbal in-deed, the predicates are but explications of the fub-jects, but they are not the lefs inftructive for being fo. He that knows all the properties of thofe individuals that have the names of man or lead, need not to be in-formed that one is an animal, and the other a metal : but it is poffible a perfon may have heard the words of animal and metal, and underftand them, and yet not

* Lee, p. 276.   † Ibid. p. 277.

have heard or underſtood the ſignification of man or lead ; and to ſuch a one this is a ſhort way of informing him, and conſequently one method of improving know-ledge.*

§ 7, *page* 192. If we invert the places of the ſub-jects in theſe propoſitions (if it be true, that every man has a notion of God, then it is the property of that idea to be formed in the minds of men : and if it be true that every man can be caſt into ſleep by opium, then that is the property of opium :) it will appear, the predicate contains no more than the ſubjects; ſo that either thoſe two propoſitions are falſe, and conſe-quently not inſtructive, or elſe they are as trifling as any before-mentioned.†

CHAP. IX.

Of our Knowledge of Exiſtence.

§ 1, *page* 186.   1. THE *eſſences* of things are only the names of that which diſ-tinguiſhes one thing from another.

2. They are not the abſtract ideas of things, becauſe there are none ſuch in the mind but of viſible ſub-ſtances.

3. They are not made by us, but only the names of them from the ſeveral qualities or properties.

4. Exiſtence is concerned in the eſſence of things, becauſe we cannot conceive the one without the other.

5. General propoſitions do not concern exiſtence, they being only the conjunction or disjunction of com-mon names given to particular things, which are ſup-poſed by the mind to exiſt.

6. Particular propoſitions, though they likewiſe concern exiſtence, yet do not declare the accidental union or ſeparation of ideas, but the real relation that

* Lee, p. 277.   † Ibid. p. 278.

is

is between substances and their modes, or between them and ourselves.*

7. The knowledge of our own existence is that of the real relation there is between a man's self and his own thoughts, and not the perception of the agreement or disagreement of ideas, because in this case there can be no ideas distinct from the person himself and his own thoughts.†

CHAP. X.

Of our Knowledge of the Existence of a God.

§ 2, *page* 188. THE author, in one of his letters to the Bishop, says, he has waved the use of the word idea in this argument, on purpose to let it into men's minds, by common words, or known ways of expression.—But I doubt a better reason might be given, viz. that the ideal phrase would render it obscure, and as far as possible make it doubtful: for

The reason why any one is convinced of his own existence, is, because he is immediately conscious of his own thoughts; but of those thoughts he can have no idea, because they neither agree nor disagree, but as the objects or cause of them do: and therefore it is this agreement or disagreement arising from the variety of causes or objects that satisfies a man of his own existence, and not the agreement of the idea of himself with the abstract idea of existence, for of that barely he would have no idea or perception at all.‡

§ 3, *page* 188. Is there any idea of nothing in a man's mind? The mind can indeed by its natural power suppose any cause to suspend or withdraw its efficacy, and by its natural powers perceive where

* Lee, p. 280.   † Ibid.   ‡ Ibid. p. 286.

there is no real cauſe operating, there can be no real effect; but by this inſtance it may appear there are principles of reaſon, where there can be no perception of the agreement or diſagreement of ideas; for no-thing is the negation of all ideas.

§ 4, *page* 189. This is an identical propoſition, and therefore trifling: for being and exiſtence is one and the ſame to the mind, with the properties of the thing exiſting; it is the ſame as to ſay, *what has its beginning from another, has its beginning from another*, and therefore the knowledge of this is not the agree-ment, &c. becauſe they are in effect but one idea; what makes it a propoſition is the mind's comparing that thing with itſelf, as it is in all certainly true, af-firmative, identical propoſitions.

§ 5, *Ibid.* But not from the agreement between the idea of himſelf and the idea of perception and knowledge; becauſe he can have no idea of percep-tion or knowledge diſtinct from the knowledge or per-ception; to know or perceive is all one, as having an idea, unleſs an idea be ſomething that is neither in nor out of the mind.

Ibid. But as we cannot ſeparate the knowledge of exiſtence from that of the things that do or have exiſted, it is the perception of real relation be-tween the things themſelves, and not the comparing the abſtract idea of one time with that of another; be-cauſe there are no ſuch ideas, they are all pure no-thing.*

---

* Lee, p. 286.

CHAP. XI.

Of our Knowledge of the Existence of other Things.

§ 3, *page* 200. **B**UT I cannot conceive how we should have either intuitive or rational knowledge without suppofing the exiftence of things without us, unlefs there could be thoughts of nothing, or reafoning about nothing.*

§ 13, *page* 207. But neither of thefe fort of propofitions can be known, but upon fuppofition of the truth of our fenfes.†

CHAP. XII.

Of the Improvement of our Knowledge.

§ 5, *page* 212. **B**UT it is as dangerous to deny all principles as to embrace falfe ones.‡

CHAP. XIV.

Of Judgement.

§ 4, *page* 224. **T**HE common account is, that knowing when it is not ufed for a fimple apprehenfion, is the perception of the neceffary or immutable relation between any things propofed to the mind. And judging is the perception of that relation between things, whether that relation be immutable and neceffary, or mutable and feparable.§

Judgement is that operation of the mind whereby we join two or more ideas together by one affirmation

* Lee, p. 302.   † Ibid. p. 293.   ‡ Ibid p. 295.   § Ibid. p. 302.

or negation ; this tree is high, that horfe is not fwift, &c. which fentences are the effect of judgement, and are called propofitions.*

C H A P. XV.

Of Probability.

§ 2, *page* 226. PROBABILITY does not fupply the defect of knowledge ; for even in the loweft degree of it, there is fome knowledge or certainty, but rather fupplies the want of evidence to make any thing fully known or certain.†

C H A P. XVII.

Of Reafon.

§ 3, *page* 242. THE common definition of reafon is, that it is the faculty in the mind which infers the truth or falfehood of any propofition by its perception of the mutable or immutable relation between the parts of that, and other propofitions with which it is compared.

The difference is, that of the four degrees or offices of this faculty, others reckon that of making the inference or conclufion to be the chief or only proper exercife of reafon.‡

Ibid. Difpofition is the ranging our thoughts in fuch order, as is beft for our own and others conception and memory. The effect of this operation is called method.§

§ 4, *Ibid.* There is no one doubts, but the queftion is, whether fuch men do not in their difcourfes make fyllogifms, though they never heard the word,

* Watts Log. p. 5.   † Lee, p. 304.   ‡ Ibid. 313.
§ Watts Log. p. 6.

or their difcourfes would not be as intelligible, or when they do not, they are not longer loofer and ob-fcurer.

§ 4, *page* 251. But in all difputations the defen-dant may be required to explain his terms, if obfcure, and fallacious, and if that be done this argument fails, or if it has any ftrength, it would be as valid againft all forts of difcourfe and conferences, for they are no lefs liable to the ambiguity of words than fyllogiftical form.*

§ 5, *page* 252. This is likewife the common prac-tice in all forts of conferences ; if any one pretends to maintain any probable propofition, he that oppofes it will make ufe of his ftrongeft arguments and attack it in the weakeft part, &c.†

§ 6, *Ibid.* *The rules of fyllogifm ferve not to furnifh the mind with thofe intermediate ideas that may fhew the connection of remote ones.*—'Tis true, he that ufes a fyl-logifm muft find out the middle term himfelf. The form of placing his words won't do that: the queftion only is, whether that which he has prepared to fay or write would not be as well or better expreffed, in as few, and that as intelligible, in the form of a fyllo-gifm, as any other form of words.‡

§ 8, *page* 254. In this fection I conceive there is a miftake about the rules of fyllogifms, and a contra-diction to his whole fcheme of abftract general ideas. For, 1ft, There are rules of fyllogifms where every propofition is particular, and the conclufion right. This paper has a plain and regular fuperficies; this pen has not fo, *ergo*, their figures are different. 2dly, If it be true, as I think it is, that every idea is a par-

* Watts Log. p. 314. † Ibid. p. 315. ‡ Ibid.

ticular exiſtence, then there can be no general abſtract ideas. If, *ex. gr.* whiteneſs and triumph be ideas, then they are ideas only of a particular white body, and a particular triumph, and therefore all that he muſt mean by general abſtract ideas, muſt be only the general names given to particulars, unleſs there could be ideas that are both general and particular, which I cannot comprehend.*

§ 14, *page* 257. Intuitive knowledge is no knowledge at all, but on ſuppoſition of the real exiſtence of things without us, which is contrary to his method and meaning.†

§ 15, *Ibid.* Nor is demonſtrative knowledge certain, but upon the like ſuppoſition.‡

§ 16, *page* 259. The author ſeems to have too much limited this faculty as he has that of rational knowledge, which is commonly extended to all ſuch knowledge which leaves no room for a rational doubt, as in the caſe of human teſtimony, when certain: of divine, when vouched by miracles.§ .

§ 20, *page* 260. When the argument is drawn from any inſufficient medium whatſoever, and yet the oppoſer has not ſkill to refute or anſwer it; this is *Argumentum ad Ignorantiam.*

§ 21, *Ibid.* St. Paul often uſes this *argumentum ad hominem* when he reaſons with the Jews, and when he ſays, I ſpeak as a man.

§ 22, *Ibid.* If an argument be taken from the nature and exiſtence of things, or addreſſed to the

* Lee, p. 316. † Ibid. p. 318. ‡ Ibid. § Ibid. p. 319.

reaſon

reafon of mankind, 'tis called *Argumentum ad Judicium*.

Befides thefe Dr. Watts reckons *Argumentum ad Fidem*, when it is borrowed from fome convincing teftimony.

Argumentum ad Paffiones, or *ad Populum*, when an argument is borrowed from any topics which are fuited to engage the inclinations and paffions of the hearers on the fide of the fpeaker, rather than convince the judgement.*

C H A P. XVIII.

Of Faith and Reafon and their diftinct Provinces.

§ 2, *page* 263. FAITH is the affent of the mind to any propofitions where the relation between its parts is not difcoverable by the ufe of our natural faculties, but the reafon of the affent is divine teftimony.

§ 3, *Ibid.* We are apt to think, that if God pleafes by immediate revelation to give to any perfons the knowledge of fuch objects or greater degrees of thofe fenfations, that he can furnifh thofe perfons with power by words or other figns to produce the like ideas or perceptions in others, which were communicated in the original revelation. But this, if granted poffible, as there is not the leaft reafon to deny, yet will not, I confefs, amount to the forming new fimple ideas; but there is no need of it, for the modes of fubftances which we know already are capable of an infinite variety in degrees and mixtures, and the words we have equally capable of being formed into an infinite number of propofitions, fo that in order to make divine or fupernatural difcoveries, there will no need of more

* Watts Log. p. 311.

organ of fenfe, of new words, or new modes of fubftances : and why God fhould not be able to reprefent a new fcene of things to the imagination, as we
find it daily by men in the defcription of foreign animals, plants, &c. is to me unaccountable. St. Paul
does not fay they were fuch degrees of pleafure that he
had no conception of, or were incommunicable to
others; but the contrary, in the words following:
God hath revealed them to us by his fpirit.*

§ 4, *page* 265. But this muft be limited to tradi-
tional revelation only, for it feems too great a reftraint
of the Divine Power to fuppofe God cannot make the
coherence of the parts of any propofition as plain to
any one's mind immediately, as by his external
fenfes, and there is no doubt but the infpired pro-
phets had as clear a view of paft and future events as
if they had feen them.†

§ 5, *page* 266. But, 1ft, It is to be confidered,
whether a perfon's own probity may not be as certainly
known to himfelf, as any ideas he can have in his
mind : or whether a perfon's knowledge that he has
the power of working miracles may not as thoroughly
convince him that his revelation comes from God, as
any rational deductions whatever can fatisfy him of any
fort of truth.

2dly. It feems derogatory to the Divine Power,
that it fhould not extend fo far as to make any thing
plain by words or other figns, by lively impreffions
upon the imagination of the perfon infpired, as the
perfon himfelf can by his own fenfes, or ufe of his natural faculties.‡

§ 6, *page* 267. But if Divine Revelation be the
only object of Divine Faith, and no revelation can be

---

* Lec, p. 324.   † Ibid.   ‡ Ibid, p. 327.

                                    fufficiently

fufficiently known to come from God but either by feeing fome infpired perfon writing, or hearing him to fpeak, or fome other perfon vouching every particular miracle, then the Holy Scriptures can afford us no fecure ground for divine faith, which is carrying the point too far : for, 1ft, It is not plain, that *faith has to do, &c.* for I cannot fee a reafon why the laws of nature may not be called divine laws, and affent given to fome propofition of divine faith, for it is fuppofed there are feveral propofitions worthy of a rational affent, and yet are the objects of a divine faith only for their being farther confirmed by revelation ; as the immortality of the foul; fo that rational affent and divine faith feem to differ only or chiefly in the degrees of evidence, and make no manner of alteration in the reafon of human actions.*

* Lee, p. 327.

F I N I S,